Mystery

Adams, Harold, 1923-

Man who missed the party

DATE DUE

JUL 6 1989	NOV 1 6 1994	
JUL 2 1 1989	AUG 3 0 1997	
AUG 4 1989	MAR 1 8 2000	
AUG 3 0 1989		
SEP 2 1 1989		
OCT 7 1989		
OCT 3 0 1989		
NOV 2 8 1989		
FEB 1 2 1990		

THE MAN WHO MISSED THE PARTY

HAROLD ADAMS

THE MAN WHO MISSED THE PARTY

THE MYSTERIOUS PRESS

New York • London • Tokyo

The Mysterious Press, 129 West 56th Street, New York, N.Y. 10019

Printed in the United States of America

First Printing: May 1989

10 9 8 7 6 5 4 3 2 1

Library of Congress Cataloging-in-Publication Data

Adams, Harold, 1923–
    The man who missed the party / Harold Adams.
    p. 192
    I. Title.
    PS3551.D367M38   1989   813'.54—dc19   88-28914
    ISBN 0-89296-252-6   CIP

To Elizabeth Terrell
Great Friend of
Cats, Carl
&
me

THE MAN WHO MISSED THE PARTY

ONE

I'd been home just over a month when Elihu had his second stroke. This time Doc Feeney got him into the Aquatown hospital for a few days and Ma at once started making plans. She's always been positive that some good comes of anything that happens and she works full-time to prove it. First she talked my North Dakota sister into letting Hank, her older son, come to Corden to finish high school. Her argument was that Elihu had to have someone reliable to help Bertha watch the hotel while Ma and Elihu were in California. That went over because neither Ma nor my sister figured I filled that bill.

Then Ma shoved Olga, our ripe and simple-minded hired girl, off on her friend, the Congregational minister's wife, and brought in Margaret to back up Bertha in the kitchen and handle the general charwoman chores. Margaret was tall, slim and sober with gray-flecked dark hair and deep brown eyes. Ma figured she was too old and straight-laced to interest me. She wore glasses that she kept shoving up with a delicate forefinger. But what impressed me most was she awed Bertha who for the first time in her life, treated her help with respect.

I tried pumping Ma about Margaret but got nothing beyond the fact she was a widow I couldn't promote. Considering her age and the schoolmarm look, the notion hadn't occurred to me until that challenge was tossed and I started looking her over with a little more care. The most I found at first was she had a very fine, full mouth and sleek hips.

The hospital stay took some starch out of Elihu. When Ma told him about the trip she had planned his first reaction was shock.

"We'll be gone for the hunting season," he told her. "You crazy, woman?"

She said that was the best reason in the world for them to be gone because he wouldn't survive if they stayed. His eyes lost their usual hawk look and he shrank some. After a while he tried to argue that he had to be around else hunters'd tear the place down and his precious son would help do the job. Ma, betraying her full life's principles, assured him I'd matured now and could accept responsibility but hurried on to tell him how she had Hank around to help and a new hired woman who was mature and reliable and of course Bertha, who'd make certain I was kept in check.

It was all so flattering to me I could hardly handle it.

The day before taking the train west, Elihu told me to bring his Dodge around front; he wanted a last look at the prairie. I said he'd be better off waiting for spring when at least the country showed some promise.

"The hell with promises," he said, "I want all the now I can hold."

So I brought the car around, helped him from the bedroom, tucked him in and started off heading west as he'd ordered.

We tootled up the hill and the minute we crested it the old man's chin came off his chest and he leaned forward with his fierce eyes glowing as he stared across the prairie with all its burned wheat and dry cornstalks bowing and swaying in the steady wind. His gnarled hands reached for the dashboard and he looked around, taking in the horizon, the near flat land and the blue sky all stretched out above.

"You know," I said, "you'd have got a hell of a lot more out of this life if you'd spent more time seeing what was out there instead of just working your ass off."

He gave me a baleful look, settled back and stared ahead.

"Sure. I could've lived like a goddamned grasshopper. Like you. Where'n hell'd that ever get you?"

"All over. And when I kick in, tomorrow or fifty years from now, I'll know I got my share of what I wanted."

He snorted. "That's fine for a bum who never wanted anything but tail. Some of us can't settle for that. I never worked for another man in my life, which is more'n you can say and you know it."

"Man, you've worked for every simple son of a bitch that walked into that hotel and bought a room for a night. You do it six days a week and most of Sunday. I think you got on the treadmill the day you climbed out of the crib."

"I done what was right, had a family, responsibility and my place in the town. What've you got? Nothing, that's what."

That all added up to nothing for both of us considering the family he had, the responsibilities he was proud of and the town he lived in. But what the hell, it was all he had so I kept my mouth shut and drove him up and down country roads while he stared at the fields, suffered for the busted farmers and tried to soak up all the sky he could see. He was all set to hate California. Nothing but goddamned hills, funny trees and crazy people.

We topped a small rise and startled a cock pheasant out of a ditch. He crossed the road before us with his stubby wings pumping like hell to keep all his fine feathers and flashy tail in the air. Seen sudden and close, he looked big as a turkey and it didn't seem possible that skinned down for dinner he didn't amount to as much as an ordinary man's bunched fist.

The old man sighed.

"Hang on," I said, "you'll hunt again."

"Shit," he said in disgust, "you never been right about anything in your life. Turn this thing around and take me home."

Hank and I saw them off in the morning. Bertha, who as far back as I can remember never left the hotel since she came to work, said her good-byes in his room alone with him and came out weeping. Ma watched her moving off, hunched over, snuffling into Elihu's handkerchief. I tried to figure Ma's expression and couldn't peg it since it seemed to fall somewhere between sympathy and satisfaction.

Her last advice to me was, don't get involved in any murders, fights or womanizing. I assured her I wasn't likely to have time but couldn't see it comforted her any. She reminded me again to leave the hired girl alone. Any female a week younger than Ma was a girl, ones twenty years younger were "girly" and she told me Margaret would cut me dead if I made any advances. I assured her the lady was too old for me and Ma came as close to snorting as her Puritan upbringing would allow.

I could tell from Hank's silence as we hiked back to the hotel he was planning how he'd control things the next few weeks. He was now a senior in high school and already planning to run for class president and probably outlining his valedictory speech for graduation in the spring. It wasn't that he was conceited, he just happened to know he was gifted, since his grandmother had drummed that into him for all his seventeen years. He also knew he had a responsibility not only to make the most of himself but to set an example for his mates. It was quite a burden to my mind but he carried it lightly.

"What're you going to do about the gambling while the hunters are here?" he asked me as we entered the lobby.

"What'd you suggest?"

"Well, since the dining room's not used nights and most of the fights in the rooms come up because some want to sleep and others want to play cards, why don't we just make them play in the dining room?"

I stared at him. "How come you knew I was planning that?"

"I didn't know," he said, waving his hand modestly. "It's just the logical thing to do. You can't stop the games, Grandma even learned that and just pretended they weren't going on because she didn't see it. But if we keep it ou. the open, you can keep it in order."

"Your confidence in me will be an inspiration all through the season. How you plan to keep our town cop under control?"

"Joey's like Grandma. He'll pretend it's not going on and won't ever come in to check."

"You thought any of setting up a blackjack game for the house, or maybe putting in a crap table?"

He barely considered it. "I don't think this crowd would go for that much."

I decided I might as well let him take over right then and went out to get coffee in the kitchen while he settled in Elihu's chair and gazed out the window, master of all he surveyed.

It looked like a trying fall. And sure enough, when I got out to the kitchen there was no coffee and neither Bertha nor Margaret was in sight.

TWO

Eric Volten, owner and chief cook in Eric's Café, greeted me with his ratchety smile and shoved a mug of hot coffee across the counter when I parked my rear on a stool before him.

"Well," he said, "the hunters'd oughta be showing up any minute now, eh?"

I tested the coffee with a spoon and nearly scalded myself.

"The reunion oughta start off with a bang," he said, leaning close. "How many of the old team you expect?"

"Got reservations for about fifteen, counting two wives."

"Uh-oh, that means thirteen from the team. Unlucky."

"There'll be at least four locals, that'll take the curse off—or make it worse, depending on your view. How many you supposed to feed at the bash?"

"Oh, maybe twenty-five. Coach Titus is staying up at the Bergstrom place. Seen him lately?"

I shook my head and risked the coffee again.

"Ain't changed a bit. Looks the same he did the first time I ever saw him, must've been thirty years ago. Same mean eyes, cold grin and sarcastic mouth. He looked fifty then, looks fifty now. Don't know if he looked old for his age then or looks young for it now."

"Well, you know how it is, folks live longer in South Dakota."

"It sure seems longer," he said. "You ain't changed either. What're you now, thirty-two?"

"Add half a dozen."

"And ten more when you're hung over, huh?"

"Maybe twenty." I didn't tell him I hadn't been hung over in two years. People don't trust reformed drunks.

He asked about Elihu and how long he and Ma'd be gone. I said not very but really thought it'd be until the old man croaked and came home for planting. I didn't want to talk about it. Eric, who's about as sensitive as a wart hog, told me he didn't think Elihu'd see another spring but he'd had a full life and what more could a man ask?

"Makes me think of the fella went to the doctor and said his eyes was botherin' him and the doc told him, hell man, if you don't stop drinking you're gonna go blind and the fella thinks that over and says, 'Well, Doc, I guess I'll keep on—I seen about everything anyway.' You think like that?"

"Never," I said, and finished my coffee, put down a nickel and stood up.

"Ever wish you coulda stayed town cop?" he asked.

"No."

"I hear you done good in Toqueville. Had the top men in town both paying you to find out the same thing. That musta been pretty good."

"Not that good. See you."

Rose, my favorite waitress, stopped me by the door and said she was sorry about Elihu and I shouldn't worry about Eric's dumb remarks, he was full of prunes. I figured it was more like he was full of what prunes produce but thanked her, patted her arm and went out into the sun.

I'd just got back to the hotel and relieved Hank of the swivel chair when a big black Olds pulled up directly in front of my window. It had dusty California plates. Two men got out. The driver moved slow and easy; a rangy man with dark floppy hair, bony shoulders and big hands. He closed the door deliberately and stared at the hotel, starting at the north corner and running his eyes across to the south end. He grinned, glanced through the window, spotted me and raised heavy eyebrows as he arched his back.

His partner, half again as wide and a couple inches taller, pulled three suitcases from the back seat, tucked one under his arm like an ordinary man'd carry a box of candy, and started for the door carrying the other two in his massive meat hooks.

I recognized the driver as Phil Jacobson, who'd played tackle on Corden's hotshot team ten years before. His giant partner was Doug Otte, who'd been right guard.

Phil opened the door for Doug and they came in, walking heavy and shrinking the lobby.

"Well," said Otte as I went around behind the counter, "if it ain't the old con, Carl. How long you been out?"

"Since about the time they let you out of the zoo," I told him.

That brought a scowl from him and a laugh from Jacobson.

"Careful, Doug," said Jacobson, "he's fast as ever. How you doin', Carl?"

"If I was doing good I wouldn't be here."

"I believe it," he said, taking the pen to sign in. "Where's Elihu?"

I told him. He moved aside to let Otte sign in and leaned on the cigar counter. "So. The prodigal son comes home and gets a hotel dumped on him. How's it feel, being in charge?"

"Bertha's in charge and she's got my nephew Hank to help. I'm just around for the grub and whatever bouncing's needed."

Otte finished signing in and I told them they'd be in room eleven; top of the stairs and back around to the left, then the door on the right.

"You better lead," I told Jacobson, "the directions are a little complicated for your buddy."

Otte glared but when Jacobson started to pick up the bags he waved him off, snatched them up and headed for the stairs. I trailed along to watch when he got to the top and sure enough, he had to wait for his partner to give him directions. I didn't laugh out loud and he had sense enough not to look down at me.

As I headed back for Elihu's chair, Boswell limped past the outside window and I opened the door for him. He grunted his thanks, heaved his old carcass over the stoop and a moment later sank with a sigh into the brown wood and leather chair just to the right of the door. I watched him fumble for his pipe, tobacco sack and matches. He couldn't find the matches so I got up and handed him a book of mine.

He'd aged since Prohibition's end. I guessed he felt it about eliminated his purpose in life, being as how for the past eleven years he'd been Corden's only bona fide moonshine man. I knew he still made some but he wasn't the county supplier anymore and couldn't feel much needed. Being modest, that didn't shrivel his soul but it did take away some of his normal energy.

I asked if he'd whipped up an extra batch of moon to have handy for the hunters. He tamped his pipe down, got the top lit, sucked some, tamped it down and lit it again. Then he shook his head.

"No need."

After a couple puffs he tilted his head toward the street behind him and asked if the California car belonged to Phil Jacobson.

"Yup."

"He bring Doug Otte?"

"Afraid so."

He looked at me with the closest thing he can dredge up that hints disapproval. The look told me not to needle the man but it also assumed I had and would.

Before the exchange got any deeper, Waterboy Wilson and Swede Eckerson came in. Waterboy had been Corden High's football team mascot. The first two years he'd never stepped on a field to do anything but deliver water during time outs. In his junior year he managed to wangle a uniform that, except for the helmet, wasn't too badly fitted. Teammates claimed he wasn't five feet tall even wearing two-inch cleats and that wasn't much of an exaggeration. He had wispy blond hair, the body of a husky baby and all the eagerness of a spaniel pup. At twenty-six, he still looked like a baby rigged out in man's clothing. Near the end of his junior year on the team he got into his first game, lost his helmet in a collision with a pulling guard, caught the runner's knee with his head and didn't see the man trip over the lost helmet because the blow knocked him cold. The runner was carried off the field with a bruised knee and sprained ankle. Waterboy was carried off unconscious.

In his senior year, during a Corden romp over Toqueville, Waterboy picked off a tipped pass in the last quarter and ran thirty-five yards for a touchdown with the entire opposition pounding behind him like a wolfpack.

Coach Titus said he was the only player alive who played in just two games and got carried off the field both times, the first one unconscious, the second in triumph.

Swede was the opposite. A tall, bony guy with red hair, he played four years on the first team, never made a touchdown or did anything that made him a hero or a goat. On the football field, like on the farm, he was steady, stubborn and dependable. He still worked for his old man and lived on the old homestead with a Norsky wife he married right out of high school. He followed Waterboy into the lobby, looking shy with his sun-bleached hair and tanned hide. His handshake was hard and dusty.

Waterboy bounced around, asking who'd come so far and wound up by the canary's cage exchanging whistles. The bird caught his excitement and fluttered around wildly chirping.

"I thought Turner'd be here by now," said Waterboy, turning toward me, "checking out the hired girl and calling everybody's wife."

"Not yet," I said.

He asked who else I was expecting and I named a few. When I said Abe Parker, he came away from the canary, grinning.

"Is Abe bringing his wife?"

I nodded.

His eyes crinkled. "No shit? Oh my God!"

"There's something I don't know?" I asked.

"There's a hell of a lot you don't know, Wilcox," he said, and laughed.

Before I could follow up on that, Jacobson and Otte came down and there was a lot of loud greeting and some horsing around until finally they took off for the beer parlor.

"What was Waterboy talking about?" I asked Boswell.

I had to depend on him for fill-ins on Corden activities that took place during my travels and stays in the likes of Stillwater Prison.

Boswell allowed as how there always seemed to be some problems when there was a pretty girl around Turner, no matter who she belonged to. He didn't offer any more details and eventually took his pipe and carcass back home. I went out to put on the feedbag with Hank in the kitchen while Margaret watched the lobby. I told Hank this was probably the last time we'd be able to share a meal till after the hunters were gone. He wanted to know why.

"Well, if what I hear about Turner's true, we won't be able to leave Margaret alone in the lobby else he'll have her ravished before we finish the first course."

Bertha snorted and said, "If she's kept you in your place over a week, she can handle any dumb jock."

I let that pass, knowing she was still in mourning for Elihu. Besides, when a cook's as good as Bertha, you tolerate a lot.

We hardly got back in the lobby before two couples pulled up in front and climbed out of a brand-new green Chevy. I recognized Abe Parker and Muggsy Bertrand. Hank trotted out to help with their luggage and followed them in.

Abe was stocky, thin-nosed, broad-cheeked and had a chin like

George Washington's. His first year on the team he'd been pounded into the ground regular as a circus tent stake, but in the next three years, according to Coach Titus, he got bigger by sheer willpower and turned out tough, quick and mean. He was called the best center in the division and won a scholarship to Iowa U, which wasn't much special then so he got no glory and wound up peddling paint for a Twin Cities company after he graduated.

His partner, Muggsy, had a chimpanzee kisser and grin. He never laughed out loud but you could about hear his smile. He played left end and was fierce on defense.

Florine, Parker's wife, was tall, slim and stylish. Her light brown hair was pressed into finger waves tight on her head like a cap. Her blue eyes brushed past me, took in the lobby with controlled distaste and returned to her woman friend, Pat.

Pat was dark, wide-eyed, wicked-lipped and lushly curved. She shot me a quick peek from under her dark bangs and I guessed she'd heard tales that made her curious. And of course I began wondering what these two would be doing while their hubbies were out murdering pheasants. Corden isn't exactly loaded with fascinating distractions.

Abe and Muggsy wanted to know who'd arrived and where they were. I pointed out they wouldn't be hard to find.

They hauled their luggage upstairs with help from Hank and promptly came back down. I could hear Florine arguing in favor of a move to Aquatown for classier rooms. Abe told her, as they reached the foot of the stairs, that she had about as good a chance of finding a room anywhere else as he had of getting elected President. She said gee, and here she'd been planning on being first lady.

They milled around in the lobby a few moments while Abe picked a couple cigars from the glass case next to the registration desk and then headed down the street.

Before they were out of sight, Margaret drifted in from the kitchen. Her usual shapeless housedress draped over her slim frame and her hair was up in a tight bun on the nape of her neck.

It gleamed, as though polished. Her high forehead, dark lashes and brown eyes didn't fit with the Puritan hair and dress. She looked around the deserted room and lifted her eyebrows.

"Everybody's off seeing the sights," I said.

"Ah. It'll be strange to have a crowd around during the weekend, won't it?"

"You ain't seen nothing yet. By tomorrow they'll be thicker than grasshoppers in a cornfield."

She strolled toward the front window and gazed out at the dusty street, where a small willawaw whipped up a tan cloud and swept it south.

"In the mood for a beer?" I asked.

She tipped her head slightly. "You offering to buy?"

"Why not?"

She looked over her shoulder and the wide mouth turned up at the corners. "You think that's a safe offer—that I wouldn't dare."

I grinned. We both knew she was right.

For a moment she considered me, then turned her head away and said, "One day I may surprise you."

She walked back through the registration alcove, passed her eyes quickly over the names entered and then went down the hall back toward the kitchen. I watched her fine hips and smooth bottom while thinking about how surprising she might be.

THREE

Turner pulled up in front a little after seven. His gleaming black LaSalle made Parker's new green Chevy look like a tin can and outshone Jacobson's Olds. Turner gave them both a glance that showed some satisfaction, then lifted a yellow leather bag from the back seat and came into the lobby.

His wavy blond hair bounced with his step and while I noticed his nose seemed bigger than I remembered, he still had the picture-model build and the easy moves of the kid who'd been every schoolgirl's dreamboy in Corden ten years before. His brown leather jacket and leather-laced boots looked casual and rich. He greeted me by name, though we'd never known each other well, and said, as he signed the register, that he was surprised to see me. "I heard you were long gone."

"Short gone," I told him. "Too short."

He grinned, glanced at names above his, dropped the pen and walked over to stare out the front window.

"Looks deader than ever," he said.

"It'll wake some by tomorrow night. You asked for room ten in your letter. You got it."

14

He turned, gave me his great grin and said fine. "Where'd the other guys go?"

"Bronco's."

"That the place used to be Gus's Cafe´?"

"Yeah. Now it's a beer parlor."

"Sounds like progress's come to Corden."

"Ma thinks it's the devil."

"She would." He laughed, took up his suitcase and headed for the stairs. "It's the last room on the left, down the east hall, right?"

"You got it."

Hank ambled in from the kitchen and I told him to take over, I was heading for Bronco's. He got his worried look, figuring I was going to get loaded with the others and I didn't reassure him any. A little healthy worry is good for his type.

I'd just reached the corner when Turner caught up with me. His hair was newly combed and he had a thoughtful look that put a strain on his smooth face.

"How come you're back in Corden again?" he asked.

"The food's good and the rent's right. What's your excuse?"

He grinned. "I was invited."

"By who?"

"Waterboy," he said, with a sidewise glance that said I wasn't to believe him. I didn't.

"I always heard you liked girls," I said.

"That's a lie. I love 'em."

He asked me how come the hotel cafe´ was closed and I said because Bertha got sick of cooking stuff she didn't give a damn about. "Now she cooks what she wants and that's fine with us."

He said he'd heard I'd been the town cop for a while and did some private detective work around the state. "Found a new career, huh?"

"Right. There's all kinds of high-powered detecting needed in South Dakota. Where you get all your gossip? And why?"

He laughed again. "Waterboy keeps me posted. I like that. I had some great days in this little old burg, days I'll never forget."

"And you've kept track of all the girls, right?"

"Yeah. They've all married or moved away."

When we reached Bronco's he opened the door and waved me in. We were smacked in the face with the sounds of the blaring juke box, laughter, talk and movement. The place stank of beer, cooked onions, tobacco and people. Everybody started for Turner at once, hollering and whooping as they gathered around. He grinned, shook hands, slapped backs and got pounded in return. Somebody started a cheer they'd yelled ten years before: "Have we got 'im? Well I guess! All Heart, All Heart, YES! YES! YES!"

Everybody wanted to buy him a beer and in seconds he had four lined up and was going to work on them with a mug in each fist. I watched him swigging while all the time looking around, his eyes shining, his face red and his golden hair mussed by women who couldn't keep their hands off him. He put down one mug, pushed the locks back with his fingers and laughed when Pat Bertrand mussed it again.

I worked my way to the bar for a beer and drifted back from the mob to look around. Pretty quick I saw the Parkers, Abe and Florine, sitting in a booth by the east wall with Muggsy Bertrand. Abe was bending over the table, talking to Muggsy. Florine watched Turner and Pat at the bar.

A hand closed on my shoulder and I turned to see Coach Titus. "Hi, Coach," I said.

"Well," he said pretending surprise, "you remember."

"Some."

He grinned and I remembered Eric's description. It was perfect. "That's what I've always liked about Carl Wilcox," he said. "No bullshit. I see you came in with the conquering hero. You two old buddies?"

"He's staying at the hotel. We just walked this way at the same time."

He nodded and asked about Elihu and Ma and we lamented old age for a few seconds. All the while he was watching Turner at the bar.

When I shut up he took a drink from his beer mug and spoke, still watching Turner.

"Know where he got the nickname Heart? I gave it to him. It was after the second game of our last season. That guy from the newspaper in Aquatown asked me, how'd we manage to whip a team that outweighed us about fifteen pounds per man and I told him it was with heart and that Harmon Turner was the shining example. I told him, 'That boy's *all* heart.' He picked that up and everybody that read him did too and I got sicker than hell of it. What the hell's he doing these days, laying rich widows?"

"I don't know. Seems to be doing okay with his fancy car and leather duds."

"Ought to be a goddamned actor in Hollywood, from the look of him. He was a helluva quarterback, though."

"How're you doing?"

"How? Or what?"

"Either. Both."

"Mostly I'm doing nothing and it's horseshit. How come you never went out for sports? You'd been a natural."

"Never liked coaches."

He laughed and it didn't seem to hurt him at all. "You were smart. Most my boys were dumber than hell. Except Dickey. Never could understand where a kid with all that muscle could come up with brains. I mean, that guy's got muscles in his shit, you know?"

"You think Turner's dumb?"

"He wasn't on a football field. But how the hell much of your life can you spend out there?"

"None of mine. Where you living now?"

"Got a place in Webster. Where all the old elephants go to die."

"Seems to me you had a little kid. A blonde girl—"

"Yeah," he said, looking away. "That was a long time ago."

"Where's she?"

"Dead." His head lifted and turned toward the bar in time to see Turner pushing toward us.

"How're you doing, Coach," said Turner, grabbing his right hand in a double grip. "You look good."

"Able to sit up and take nourishment," said Coach, lifting the beer in his left hand.

"You always claimed that stuff'd kill me."

"It will. But then, you never did want to live forever, did you?"

"Damn right. You know, I remember just about everything you ever told me, and some you told the others. We had us a helluva football team, right?"

"It was for a year, but that was a long time ago."

Some of the glow left Turner's eyes. "Well, we've always got it."

"Yeah, for whatever that's worth. What're you doing now?"

Turner waved his hand and I realized he hadn't brought a beer with him. "Insurance. You retired?"

I drifted away from them and eased toward the Parker and Bertrand booth. Pat was back beside her husband and Parker was looking restless.

"We'd ought to be getting up a poker game," he told me the moment I was close enough to hear. "We gonna play in room two?"

"In the dining room."

"Oh ho! When the cat's away, huh?"

"Just keep the noise down so we don't wake Joey."

There was a sudden stir at the entrance and everybody looked around to see Bull Dickey arrive with his sidekick, Ed Folsum. Bull had a neck thicker than most men's thighs and an anvil chin, the chest and ass of a gorilla and deep-set, thoughtful eyes. Even at my height I could see his big head over the crowd as he worked toward the bar. Muggsy got up and his wife asked where he was going.

"Wanna talk to Bull," he answered. "You gonna come along and muss his hair?"

"I can't reach that high, and besides, he's not cute."

"Not many of us are," said Muggsy as he pushed through the crowd.

Parker glowered a moment at Pat, then turned to me and groused that all this crap with old heroes was putting off poker.

"How about you pass the word a game'll be starting in fifteen minutes back at the hotel?"

"What're we supposed to do?" demanded Florine.

"You can go and hang on old Heart Turner."

I slipped off to round up poker players and about ten minutes later five of us started toward the hotel, leaving Pat and Florine sulking in their booth. When I glanced back just before going out, I saw Turner heading their way.

One game was already under way when we arrived in the dining room. I recognized a couple faces but didn't remember any names. Margaret had supplied a pitcher of ice water and glasses so the guys could mix their bourbon and water. I sat with Parker and three hunters I remembered as lousy players from years before. It was a nickel ante, quarter limit raise game and about as quick as a skunk can lift his tail I was out three bucks and gave my place to Muggsy, who drifted in looking sour.

Back in the lobby I relieved Hank and suggested he keep an eye on the game. That suited him. He always thought he could learn something watching men make fools of themselves and there was plenty of that in any poker game.

A few minutes after nine o'clock, five guys came in a group and their leader told me they had a reservation. I didn't like his snotty style the moment he opened his mouth but the reservation was there and I gave him room two, which was the only one in the place big enough to hold his crew. The snotty one signed in as Bud Kinman, of Detroit, and he told me they wanted a call at 4:45 A.M.

"The birds won't be up," I said.

"Well, you do your job and we will be, okay?"

"My job doesn't run twenty-four hours a day."

"Okay, have the cook make the call. We won't be eating here so she won't have to do anything else for us."

"You want lunches?"

"Naw, I know where we can get good ones."

Sure, I thought, you'll stop by Paris.

I told him where the room was and he asked wasn't I going to haul up their bags and I said no we were shy on help and long on business and he looked healthy enough to help himself.

We parted the best of enemies.

My next customer was alone and without a reservation but I had the windowless, unnumbered storeroom available and stuck him in there, warning that he'd probably get a roommate before the night was over. He said that was okay if it wasn't a bedbug. Real hunters will settle for space on the balcony outside if we don't get sleet.

By ten-thirty the poker players were getting a little loud and I drifted over to the door for a look. Two of the strangers had left Parker's table, which now had Muggsy, Waterboy, Swede and Doug Otte. Otte, I remembered, usually lost and it made him sociable as a grizzly with fresh cubs. Waterboy, also as usual, was winning and crowing. He kept telling Otte how dumb he'd played his last hand. Finally Otte leaned forward and told him to goddamned shut up or he'd close his yap for him.

"Go on," yelped Waterboy, "you mess with me and I'll climb your frame and chew your ear to a rag."

Everybody laughed the way they always do when the little man talked tough and of course that made Otte madder than ever. I eased around close to his side and he flashed me his mean look.

"Stay outta this, old con, or you'll get hurt," he told me.

"You can't take the losses," I said, "get out of the game."

It was the wrong thing to say and I knew it but could no more keep it down than squelch a hiccup. He made the mistake of reaching for me before he was on his feet. I grabbed his arm as he rose, spun him around, slapped on a hammerlock and as he went up on his toes, slammed my knee into his butt. It lifted him off the floor with both feet up and I let him drop. The crash shook the whole hotel and didn't help his tailbone any.

I waited for his head to rise and cocked my right as Bull Dickey slipped between us and put his hammy hand on Otte's shoulder.

"Take it easy," he said, "that was a bad slip. You might have hurt yourself."

"I'll kill 'im," gasped Otte, "so help me—"

"You'll need plenty of help," crowed Waterboy.

Bull turned to him and said, "Lay off, okay?"

Waterboy grinned but shut up. I moved back while Bull got Otte to his feet. His face was white and sweaty, his eyes wild. He glared at Waterboy and looked around for me but Bull carefully steered him toward the hall, talking low and Otte apparently decided he wasn't in shape for round two and went peacefully.

Muggsy, who was at my side, shook his head.

"You just don't give a damn how big they are, do you?"

"I give a damn, you bet."

He shook his head again. "No, the bigger they are, the better you like it."

The fracas had broken Parker's concentration on poker and he suddenly looked around and asked where the hell his wife was.

Muggsy looked blank.

Parker glared at him and then they both headed for the door. I thought of trailing along but figured it was none of my business and told Hank he'd ought to hit the sack since he had an early call to make. He didn't faint when I told him the hour but turned a little pale and headed upstairs.

About ten minutes later I saw the two couples coming past the corner gas station. Nobody was talking. The women walked together in front with the guys close behind. Muggsy nodded at me as they passed by in the lobby. None of the others gave me a glance. A little later I could hear some unfriendly discussion going on in room nine but it ended soon.

I closed the gambling room at twelve without any trouble and by twelve-thirty was settled on the parlor couch fairly satisfied with myself and the day.

FOUR

Just as I was drifting off to sleep the front door opened and closed quietly. I waited for steps to approach the stairs but heard none and after a few seconds rolled to my feet, slipped into my shoes and went out to the lobby.

Heart Turner was sitting on Elihu's swivel chair, staring out at the feebly lit street. I walked over to the rocker near him and sat down. He didn't turn his head but after a few seconds spoke.

"You know, it's not much of a town."

"So why'd you come back?"

He shook his head. In the dark its golden gleam was lost.

"You remembered it as better?" I asked.

"I didn't remember it real." He turned the chair to face me. "How come you always come back?"

"Maybe because every time I leave it makes me feel so good I have to come back and do it again."

He combed his hair back with his fingers. "You're always a kidder, aren't you? Ever figure you're kidding yourself?"

"All the time."

He turned back to the street. I looked too and thought how

quiet it is when the crickets are gone and the furnace is at rest below. There was no wind from the prairie and folks upstairs had finished with the bathroom and bed movements. When I shifted to reach my cigarette makings the wooden chair creaked loudly.

"You ever have a job you liked?" he asked.

I thought some and guessed part of the cowboying had been fun, riding broncs and watching the sky, going to town on weekends. Of course most of it was lousy. I'd liked learning how to paint signs when Larry Myers taught me the tricks and we traveled together. He wore comfortable as old boots.

"What you really liked, then, was traveling with the guy, it wasn't messing around with letters and paints, it was the laughs."

"It was mostly that, but doing a job right, in your own time and style, that was good too. I guess the most was that all the time we worked together I knew he wasn't going to live long and I worked at giving us both a good time because I knew it wouldn't last."

Turner shook his head and leaned his elbows on his knees.

"I can't think of one damned thing I want to do that'll make me money. Not one. If I could've done it playing ball and done it good, I'd have been so damned happy I wouldn't've cared if I died in the last game. I'd've died happy."

"You don't like insurance?"

He gave a nasty laugh. "Carl, I was one lousy month with the insurance company. Couldn't read one of their damned policies without falling asleep. The most boring thing in the world is talking to people about how they should look out for their damned families and all that stuff. Nobody my age wants to hear they're not going to live forever. So for a while I sold clothes. The only good thing about that was the twenty percent discount. I was able to buy all the junk I wanted when I was in high school. But that's a shitty way to live too, always waiting around for somebody to come in and nothing to do but straighten up stuff people've come in and pawed over. It's an ass-kissing job, you know? 'Hey, you look great in that,' or 'You got good taste, that brown and green polka dot tie's gonna knock the girls out.' I sold liquor too. That's a job for drunks. I can't find a damned thing I want bad enough to work for and I'm just letting my life go to hell."

"I'd play 'Hearts and Flowers,' " I said, "only it doesn't go too hot on a mouth organ."

He hunched his shoulders irritably and scowled. "You just don't understand."

"Yeah I do. You were a hero when you were a kid and you thought it'd last forever. I was a bum when I was a kid and that does last forever. You want a smoke?"

He suddenly grinned and shook his head. "No. Cuts your wind. I need all I can get."

He stared out the window once more while I lit up.

"Bugs're gone," he said, squinting up at the streetlight. "Remember when moths used to bang around the kerosene lamps and get in the chimney and char all black? I knew a girl once, told me I was like them. Beating my brains out trying to swallow the light. Imagine a girl telling you a thing like that?"

"Who was she?"

"Just a girl. Read a lot. All her reading never gave her a notion how I should make out as a man. I figured, back then, if I played well enough everybody'd know about me and things'd take care of themselves. It sure took care of the girls back then. I didn't have to tell them how great they were or buy 'em presents or take 'em places that cost money. They told *me* how great I was. Didn't have to say much, it was in the way they looked at me and what they'd let me do, you know?"

I didn't but nodded and smoked my cigarette.

He abruptly stood. "Hey, how about we take a walk?"

"Where?" I said, but I knew.

"Fairgrounds. Just go out there and take in the field where we played in front of the stands there. You're not sleepy, come on."

We went. There was a chill in the air that lifted his chin and puffed out his chest. He stared at the star-bright sky that got still

lighter as we reached the town's edge and walked along the
narrow road to the grounds on the rim of the prairie. The wind
came out of the north, not mean yet, but strong enough to send
a big tumbleweed rolling ahead of us, heading toward a gathering
of mates at a fence lining the south grounds.

"Reminds me of that old song, 'Tumbling Tumbleweed.' " he
said. "It used to make me think of you, the bum that traveled all
over and did crazy stuff. When I heard you'd been put in prison
it seemed like the most godawful thing in the world. Did you
know my old man?"

"Only by sight."

"He inherited a claim from my uncle a long time back. This
uncle got kicked by a cow named Peg and got creeping paralysis,
which finally killed him. Anyway, my old man took over his
farm and after a while Ma left the house one morning and never
came back. I wasn't more'n a baby and the old man couldn't
handle me and the farm so he moved to town and got a job at the
grain elevator. Hated it. He'd loved the goddamned prairie and
felt like he was in prison. Got cancer and died while I was in
junior high. Never saw me play one football game."

He laughed. "Not that he'd've given a damn. Thought games
were a waste of time. Probably right but I'm damned glad I didn't
grow up on the farm and never get a chance to play."

We climbed into the grandstand and sat on benches overlooking the big oval spread east of us. He leaned forward, propping
his hands on the bench.

"When I was little I figured it was my fault Ma walked off. My
grandma, Pa's mom, said the wind did it. 'Prairie wind,' she told
me, 'addles women's minds.' I asked how come it didn't addle
men's and she said because they were born addled and never
knew the difference."

He was quiet awhile, staring down at what had been a football
field, but his mind wouldn't stay on it.

"I don't guess Pa was very smart. He didn't talk to me or
anybody else I know of. I wonder how guys like him get around

to marrying. I guess women sort of herd them into it while they're busy thinking about planting corn or something. I could never imagine him with a hard-on. You ever think of yours that way?"

"No."

He laughed. "Crazy, isn't it? Nothing seems worse than your own ma and pa doing what you wish you were doing most of the time."

I didn't laugh and he got embarrassed and shut up. After a while he got up, so did I and we walked to the end of the seats and down to the ground. He looked at his watch and shook his head.

"Nearly one. Christ. You gonna make wake-up calls?"

"Hank will."

"I hate hunting. Just a lot of damned hiking around over plowed fields and fighting through corn rows and killing birds that're prettier than hell. Most guys get kicks out of hitting them with the old buckshot, seeing feathers fly and birds drop. It makes me sick."

"Why'd you come?" I asked. "You hate hunting, don't like the town—"

"Memories," he said, mockingly. "All the great people and the old teammates, the bullshit—"

"And the girls."

He flipped his right hand. "All the girls I knew are gone or married or both. Look around you, you see any? Come on, I'll walk you back to the hotel."

"I can find my way alone if you're planning something."

He looked up at the stars and shook his head. "Just gonna walk. Never get sleepy till dawn."

He stayed with me back to the hotel and stood a moment by the front door.

"You know," he said, "it may sound nuts, but I always envied you. You never gave a damn what anybody thought, went your own way, never depended on any damn body."

"Who'd you ever depend on?"

"Jesus. *All* of them. The team, the fans, the friends and the girls. That sound dumb to you?"

"No, I see what you mean. You always got your charge from the crowd."

"It's the love," he said and laughed again. "Hey, I'll see you tomorrow."

He looked at his watch and took off with his springy walk. I went inside and hit the couch.

FIVE

I woke uneasy, like a drunk coming to and worrying about what he might've done the night before that'll cost him today. Only I'd gone to bed sober so what was wrong?

I struck a match and looked at my pocket watch. It said five-thirty. I'd slept four hours.

Then I became aware of the sound upstairs. Some damned fool was taking a shower. I settled back and closed my eyes but sleep didn't come.

I rolled out, dressed, tried to appreciate my clear head and steady stomach and even thought of going after a cup of coffee but decided I wasn't brave enough to enter Bertha's kitchen before six. I went to the hallway door and listened to the shower. It ran steady as a fountain in a park, which was unnatural. There should be splashing and splattering.

I hiked up the creaking steps, noticing that the rubber runners were worn through at the center, reached the top and looked toward the shower room. Elihu had run the partition on the north side only up within two feet of the ceiling and light from inside spread overhead across the hall. I moved closer, listening and heard nothing but the steady drumming of the shower stream.

Steps approached from the west and I turned to see Bull Dickey's frame filling the hall. He wore a navy blue robe and a scowl that'd scare a drunk Marine.

"That's been running half an hour," he told me. "It's driving me nuts."

"Sure it's been that long?"

"I took a leak at five. It was running then."

I hammered the door. No response. I looked at Bull. He stepped to the door, put his shoulder against it, crouched a little, then heaved. The door popped open with a crack like a rifle shot and slammed against the inside wall. We both went in and approached the closed shower curtain. I pulled it back. The white body below glistened under the pouring water and the cement floor was clean but my eye caught the splash of red on the shower wall where the water didn't hit. The stain was turning dark at the top and disappeared near the floor. Turner's blond hair was plastered on his smooth skull and quivered like something alive under the stream from above.

I shut it off and turned to Bull.

"I've gotta call Joey. Will you stick around and keep people out till I get back?"

He stared down at the body. "It's Turner."

"Yeah."

"Damn. Yeah, I'll watch."

The popped door had brought people into the hall. I saw Muggsy Bertrand in striped pajamas and Phil Jacobson with red pajama tops, hunting pants and boots. Neither of them looked fresh. I told everybody there'd been an accident and we'd get things sorted out if they'd just go back to their rooms and take it easy.

Nobody went. I pushed through and ran down the stairs to the telephone. I got Doc Feeney first, then Joey. Neither of them seemed either surprised or grateful for the early attention, both said they'd come quick.

Joey was first. Ever since I'd filled in for him the winter before he'd been quicker than a bluejay on the job so nobody'd ever suggest I take over permanently.

He got down on his knees and lifted Turner's head long enough to examine the down side. I couldn't see what he did but could tell from his expression he was shaken.

"What?" I asked.

He looked up. "There's a hole in his temple. You hear a shot?"

"There wasn't any shot," said Bull. "I've been awake since five and there wasn't any noise like that."

Joey got up with a grunt and stared gloomily around the small shower room. When he spotted Turner's pajamas and robe hanging on the door hook he started toward them.

"I checked," I said. "Nothing in the pockets but a hanky in the robe."

"Man's?"

I shook my head.

He took the handkerchief out and spread it on his big hand. It was pale purple with white lace edging. No initials. Joey folded it carefully and stuck it in his shirt pocket.

Doc Feeney bustled in past the hall crowd, handed Joey his topcoat and me his suit jacket, tugged up his pants at the knees and crouched over the body. He was puffing. Water dripped from the shower head and splashed on the dead man's white hip.

After a few seconds Doc rose, pulled his hanky from a back pocket and wiped his hands while still staring at the body near his feet.

"Incredible. The hole suggests a slug big as a forty-five, but it didn't go through." He looked around the room and up at the space open along the partition top. "He'd have to have been shot at practically point-blank range."

"That's what I figured," said Joey. "The door was bolt-locked from inside."

"Well, all I know right now is, he's dead. Probably has been for about an hour."

Joey stared down at him. He looked quite a ways because

Doc's only five five and Joey's over six feet. Doc has a black goatee everybody claims is dyed, a razor-sharp mustache, a round, smooth skull with a fringe of short-trimmed black hair. Joey's shapeless mug is seamed and jowly; his graying hair always needs a trim.

While Doc got back into his suit and topcoat we discussed the murderer's access. They both figured what Doc called "the miracle weapon" had been fired from the top of the partition by someone standing on the bureau outside. It was also possible, they both admitted when I suggested it, that someone had come through the unlocked door, did the deed, locked the door, hauled himself over the partition and dropped to the floor outside or went down the bureau.

"Only I don't know many but you that're monkey enough for that kind of stunt," said Doc.

"We got a hotel full of athletes," I reminded him.

"Well, I'm sure Joey appreciates your simplifying the problem for him. I'll leave it to you, including the delivery of the body to my office for an autopsy."

By the time that was taken care of most of our guests were in the dining room, where Margaret and Hank were busy delivering Bertha's blessings to the chomping crowd.

Back when Bertha decided we'd close the dining room, Elihu had agreed on condition she'd serve breakfasts during hunting season and put up lunches for guys that wanted them.

Joey and I had coffee in the kitchen with a couple doughnuts each and then went out into the dining room to look over our suspects. I guessed there were thirty people, which didn't include some who were still in the sack and maybe half a dozen who'd moved out already for God knew what.

Most eyes were on Joey from the moment we walked through the kitchen door and it only took a couple throat clearings by him to silence the mob.

He told them what they already knew and asked if anyone had

heard any unusual sounds during the night or morning. That brought a general murmur but no information.

"Okay," said Joey. "I'm asking the football reunion crowd to stick around awhile. I know you're all anxious to get out on the hunt but I know you all want this awful thing straightened out quick as possible and I need your help. Okay?"

Most were willing or pretended to be. I saw a couple sour looks but nobody was dumb enough to object out loud.

Just as Joey began explaining his system for questioning folks, Waterboy came charging in through the lobby door. He spotted Joey and trotted up to him.

"Is it true—has Turner been murdered?"

"Looks like," nodded Joey. "Won't be sure till Doc finishes his autopsy."

Waterboy spun around and stared belligerently at the crowd. He took in Jacobson, Ed Folsum, Abe Parker and Florine, Muggsy and Pat had finally Bull Dickey. They all looked tired and a little mussed except Florine. Her hair was glossy, her face powdered, rouged and lipsticked like she was expecting photographers. I wondered if she expected reporters from the city.

Joey leaned over as Waterboy whispered to him, then nodded and said it'd be a good idea if he'd go get Swede and anybody else around who'd known Turner well. The little man took off, looking grim and important.

Joey walked with me to the lobby and read the registrations we'd had so far for the weekend. It didn't seem to tell him any more than it had me but he kept staring until I suggested we'd ought to search the rooms and cars.

"What'd you figure we'll find?"

"Maybe a cannon with a silencer, an airgun or a slingshot."

He sighed, said okay and went to call his deputy, Tim Spratt. Tim was a sometimes carpenter and handyman who once worked for Elihu. The old man had thrown him out, saying he couldn't drive a nail straight or follow a saw line but he worked cheap and now almost made a living doing odd jobs for widows. He loved being Joey's deputy, wearing a gun and carrying a nightstick. He came on the run and looked pretty down when Joey explained he was to stand guard in the lobby and keep his eye on both exits, the one at the foot of the stairs and the other in the lobby.

"What if somebody sneaks down the fire escape in back?"

"Hank'll be watching there. You stay in sight here so people'll know the law's in charge, okay?"

That put a different light on things. Tim said great and took up his station by the front door facing the northside exit.

"Watch for anybody carrying anything out and ask to see if it looks suspicious," Joey told him.

"Like what?"

"Like anything but a bag lunch or a flask."

I assigned Hank to the back watch and then Joey and I started going through the rooms. We had twenty-three regulars, the converted storage room, two apartments upstairs and four on the first level. None of the first-level apartments were interconnected so they didn't seem likely for weapons stashing.

We started the search in Turner's room because Joey figured that would be the cutest place for the killer to hide his weapon. It was a surprise to both of us that Turner'd been neater than a house-proud clubwoman. His shaving gear was spread on the glass shelf over the sink as clean and bright as a window display. His suitcase stood on the bench at the foot of the bed with its top up and the clothes folded perfectly inside.

Joey moved around, lifting things carefully and putting them back as if Turner might show up and be offended if anything looked disturbed. I found nothing in the bureau drawers but the Gideon Bible, which sat in the right-hand corner of the first top drawer where Ma always had our hired girls put it. Every so often she checked to see if anybody moved one. Since she never said anything about what she found I guessed she was usually disappointed.

I made a point of always putting my copy on top of the bureau and the hired girls put it back inside each morning. Ma knew better than to ask why I moved it, she figured it'd only bring some smart, sacrilegious crack and early on it would have. But I think she got some satisfaction from the fact I handled the book daily and felt deep down it might have an effect. I never begrudged her that small comfort.

Joey'd been so careful of the suitcase I didn't think he could've found anything but a cannon so I did a recheck and came up with an envelope tucked between his shoes and the suitcase side.

"What's that?" asked Joey as I slipped a single sheet of blue paper out of an envelope.

"Letter from a woman," I said, handing it over. He squinted at the fine script and gave it back, asking me to read it. He didn't like anything not in print.

" 'Dear Heart,' " I read. " 'It was real nice to get your call and quite a surprise since I had not had one word for years so how come you did not think I might be married or something? You think everybody else's life stops because you left town? Well, in my case you are right but I am not sure I want to go back to what was because I know it will not come to anything again and I cannot stand that kind of letdown. Maybe I will see you when you come and maybe I will not.

" 'I will tell you what. Write me a nice letter and tell me what you plan and what you want of me and if you do it right, I will think about it. You have never written one word to me and I want a letter and if I do not get what I want then you will not get what you want. So do not come to town expecting me to fall in your lap like all the other gaga girls you always had even though I have always loved you and always will. Forever.' "

Joey took the blue slip back and scowled.

"She didn't sign it. Know who it is?"

My headshake was a lie. I had a strong notion.

"Damn funny she didn't sign it."

I thought so too.

He shook his head. "No date. No return. You figure he answered it?"

"I'm not sure he could write."

"Oh, he could do that. He wouldn't've got out of Corden High without he learned that much."

He put the letter back in its envelope and gently returned it to the suitcase. After a final look around he said we'd go across the hall to room nine.

Florine answered his knock.

"Excuse me," said Joey in his soft-edged voice. "We need to go through everybody's things. Just routine, you know—"

"Has somebody been telling you tales?" demanded Florine, glaring at me. "You think Abe'd do anything to Heart Turner?"

"I got no tales and no notions," said Joey, "I just got to check everything. We been through Turner's stuff across the hall, we're checking here next and this's all a hell of a chore, if you'll pardon me, ma'am, and I'd like to get through it quick as possible."

The edge on his voice hardened as he spoke and thought of his belly with only doughnuts in it. Florine backed off, apologized and asked if he wanted her to stay while he looked.

He said yes and recovered his usual manners, saying she had the room looking so neat and fine he felt bad poking around.

"Well," she said, brightening up, "I can't stand living out of suitcases. Every time I go to a hotel I right away unpack and use the bureau drawers and try to be like at home. I think people who don't are just plain lazy, don't you?"

Joey assured her she was right and obviously a great homemaker and they got so cozy I started plotting ways to make her mad again.

She tried to watch both of us at once as we poked around but concentrated mostly on me. Joey went through the drawers, starting at the top, where I got a glimpse of pink underwear which must've been stacked over the Bible and wished Ma could see that. She'd throw a fit. He moved quickly from there to the next drawer where he found shirts and felt free to paw through. I drifted over to the wall pegs and checked out the pockets in a suit hung there and the hunting jacket. Feeling something hard I

reached in the right-hand pocket of the jacket and pulled out a
sheath knife. The blade was freshly sharpened and gleamed in the
light from the east window.

"I thought Turner was shot," Florine said with some heat.

"Don't know for sure," I said, shoving the blade back in the
sheath. "All we know for sure is he's dead and there's a head
wound."

Joey shoved the bottom drawer shut and turned to Florine.

"Your husband ever talk any about Turner?" he asked.

"Not particularly." She said that with care while watching his
face. She tried to avoid looking my way. I asked if it was okay
for me to look in their suitcases and she waved me toward where
they were parked under the bed.

"You know Turner before this reunion?" asked Joey.

"Yes, as a matter of fact, I did. We met in the Cities. I suppose
you'll hear about it so I may as well put things straight right now.
He found me attractive and he made a rather obvious pass and
Abe got mad and there was nearly a fight but it didn't amount to
a hill of beans and Abe's not the type to brood over a thing like
that and he's never owned a pistol in his life. The only gun he's
got is that shotgun which is out in the car and was there all night
and would wake the dead if he shot it in that shower room— "

"It wasn't done with any shotgun," said Joey as he went over
to the bed and felt under the pillows. "Did you kind of go for
Turner?"

"I *liked* him, yes. He was a very attractive and charming
fellow. But I never got involved in anything with him and Abe
knows that. I mean, if he felt there was anything serious going on
between us you don't think he'd have come to this reunion, do
you?"

Joey felt under the mattress without answering. I found the
suitcases empty. Not a dust mote or a stray hair. I closed them up
and shoved them back under the bed.

"He was a wonderful dancer," said Florine. "We danced just
once. That time when he made the pass. He enjoyed the dance so

much he just sort of kissed me as a, you know, thank you. That's all it was, an impulsive thing that didn't mean anything at all and I convinced Abe of that."

Joey stood erect and looked around once more.

"He ever call you on the telephone?" he asked.

"No," she said quickly. "Why'd he call me?"

"Things like that happen. Well, thanks a lot. Is Abe down in the lobby?"

"He was still in the dining room when I left."

Joey thanked her again and we went into the hall.

"Fine-looking woman," he said softly after the door closed.

"I didn't think you noticed stuff like that."

"Just because I don't chase 'em like you, don't mean I don't look. Abe signed in for the both of them, didn't he?"

"Uh-huh. You want her to write a note so you can check the hand?"

"It might come to that."

He stopped outside the shower room partition and stared up at the opening.

"It makes most sense that whoever done it was up on top of the bureau there. Man's hardly ever more helpless than in a shower or a bath."

I could think of at least one more vulnerable position but didn't mention it.

He moved closer to the bureau, which came about to his titty height and turned to me.

"If you were gonna take a crack at somebody in there, how'd you do it?"

I stared at him.

"Come on," he said, "I know you didn't do anything like that—if you were sore at him you'd've just socked him. All's I want to do is see how a spry man'd go up."

I took off my shoes, heisted myself with a jerk, caught the bureau edge with my foot and stood erect. It put my shoulders just under the partition edge.

"Can you reach over?" he asked.

I went on my toes and demonstrated yes. It wasn't easy, but I could manage. I guessed he was thinking a tall woman could do it too.

"How come Elihu didn't run the partition to the top?" he asked.

"Probably wanted circulation so the shower wouldn't get mold. Or maybe he had short two-by-fours and wanted to save money."

He chuckled. "Old Elihu, he thinks of everything."

"Everything but having a good time."

"You don't know what good times he had before he married and had you kids."

"The hell I don't. His idea of a good time was always working his ass off."

I got down and put my shoes back on.

SIX

We went down the south hall and turned west to room two. It was the biggest in the hotel with two double beds and space enough for two cots during pheasant season. This was where Bud Kinman and his crew had parked for the night. The room was a mess with clothes on the straightbacked chairs, cigar butts and ashes in and around the ash trays, a few beer bottles on the floor and pulp Westerns and *Spicy Detective*s on the bureau.

"They got off early," said Joey.

"Left while we were messing in the shower."

"Any of 'em know Turner?"

"Doesn't seem likely. They come from Michigan."

We went through the mess and found nothing worth noticing.

Otte was alone in room eleven, stretched out on the bed with two pillows under his head.

"You busted my goddamned tailbone," he told me. "I checked with Doc Feeney."

"He put a cast on it?" I asked.

"You'd have a cast on your head if I could move worth a shit—"

"Where's Phil Jacobson?" asked Joey, the eternal peacemaker.

"Downstairs. You won't find anything here but long johns and wool socks. Our guns're down in the car."

Joey nodded, asked if it was okay for us to look around and Otte waved his hand generously.

"You know any guys besides Abe Parker that got a reason to be mad at Turner?" asked Joey as he pulled open the top bureau drawer.

"Come on, Joey, you know damned well Abe didn't kill anybody. He's a hothead but never carried a grudge in his life. I played on the same team with him four years and by God, I know the kind of man he is."

Joey poked under the spare blanket in the bottom drawer and straightened up slowly.

"You like Turner?"

"In a game I loved the son of a bitch. He made it go, you know? All hopped up and tougher than owl shit. Only thing wrong with Turner off the field, he couldn't think of anything but nooky. Of course the rest of us were about as bad, except maybe Bull, but none of us had his balls. He was the horniest son of a bitch you ever saw." He thought about that a second and lifted his chin toward me. "Almost as bad as your horny little sidekick here."

"Don't call me little," I told him. "You'll get the other end busted. It's thicker but I could manage."

He laughed and shook his head. "Wilcox, if you weren't so small you'd never have lived. The girls think you're cute and the guys are ashamed to bash you 'cause it'd get 'em no credit. If you were bigger, somebody'd have killed you by now."

"You going to hunt?" asked Joey, trying to change the subject.

"Oh hell yes. You know how it is with us football players. Used to playing hurt. All I got to do is stay off my ass."

I told him everybody loved a hero and he laughed again. It seemed like when he wasn't playing poker he managed to keep his sense of humor.

The Bertrands weren't in twelve so we walked in and pawed
through their stuff. Pat wasn't neat as Florine; all their clothes
were still in suitcases packed about as orderly as a laundry bag.
Her underwear was silk with white lace trim and it embarrassed
Joey but he was getting bold by now and went through it all
thoroughly. On the bureau I found a double picture frame with
snapshots of two kids, about four and five. There was a
dark-haired girl standing pigeon-toed with her head down and her
hands clasped behind her back. Her brother, who was smaller,
leaned into her side and stared at the camera with suspicious
eyes.

Back in the hall I reminded Joey we still had to look through
car trunks.

"This whole thing is a mess," he complained. "There's too
blamed many people around. We won't find a damned thing."

"It'll narrow down when we talk to them. Murder's usually
close to home."

"Yeah, but none of these folks're home."

I'd put Bull Dickey and Ed Folsum in fourteen. Actually, of
course, it was thirteen, which hadn't been too lucky for some but
had been fine for me back when Kitty stayed in it. Bull and Ed
were downstairs with nearly everybody else so we were able to
look over their stuff in jig time and found just as much as in the
other rooms.

We finished the search upstairs and moved down to the cars.
That took a while because there was some messing around
finding car owners to unlock trunks. We found one four-ten, lots
of twelve gauges, a few sixteens, double and single barrels, an
over-and-under and about everything but a sawed-off. Phil
Jacobson had a fancy job with scrolls and trim but most of the
guns were working tools. Everybody had ammunition to spare.
Nobody had a handgun, airgun or crossbow.

Back in the lobby Joey asked the reunion crowd to stick around
a while longer and that brought a few mutters but no argument.
We went into the dining room, which had been cleared by

Margaret and Bertha, took a booth near the kitchen, got coffee
and were starting a schedule for questioning the gang when Bull
Dickey came in and asked if it was okay for a few guys to start
a poker game in the booth by the east wall. Joey okayed that.
Margaret came by to ask did we want some breakfast and Joey
wrestled the notion a moment and lost. He felt we'd ought to tend
to business. I said I'd take another doughnut. I eyed Margaret's
bottom when she moved off, and Joey asked what I knew about
her.

"She's a widow from Iowa and she's got Bertha eating out of
her hand."

"Turner pay her any mind?"

"Never saw her, far as I know."

"Tall for a woman," he said.

"You figure she could reach over the partition?"

"Kitchen crew gets up early, right?"

"Nobody working for Bertha goes wandering off to kill
guests."

"It doesn't seem likely," he admitted.

Somebody hustled into the dining room through the lobby door
and I looked over to see Mayor Syvertson heading toward us.

"You deputized Carl yet?" he asked Joey.

"I got a deputy."

"But Carl's had experience with murders—"

"I got a hotel to worry about," I said, "and in case you haven't
noticed, it's full of people."

"Hank and Bertha can handle it with that new woman—now I
can see you're helping already so we'd ought to make it official."

Joey patiently explained that this murder was only a few hours
old and might be solved in the next few so there was no reason
to get in a tizzy yet.

The mayor decided to allow him that and asked who we were
going to question now? Joey stared at him, as eager for his help
as I'd been the winter before, sighed and turned to me.

"Let's start with Abe Parker. Carl, will you go get him? Then just keep an eye on the folks out there. I'd appreciate it."

. So I got Abe, went into the kitchen and told Bertha her dining room was closed and she let me know *she'd* decide about that and did and the questioning began.

I retreated to the lobby, where Hank met me and said we had to get the shower door repaired.

"I thought you'd have it fixed by now," I said.

"The wood's all shattered where the lock goes."

So I took the old door from the linen closet, planed it down some and hung it on the shower opening. It had a gap of an inch and a half top and bottom that didn't hurt anybody. Margaret fixed up a curtain to hang over the open linen closet entry.

Meanwhile Hank hauled hot water up to rooms so guys could shave by their bureaus in the big white bowls before the tall mirrors. Most of the time there was a line waiting for the toilet. I suspected there was going to be a lot of constipation around the place.

Florine asked me if it was okay for her and Pat to park in the parlor away from all the bustle and men in the lobby and I said fine. Later I found them playing cribbage on a side table they'd cleared. Florine managed to look embarrassed at being caught playing cards on Sunday but Pat only grinned.

About eleven the rain began. It slapped against the north windows and wall and flowed down the glass so fast you could hardly see into the street. The real hunters in the lobby looked glummer than ever because they figure the rain keeps pheasants down longer and gives them a better shot when the birds are forced up, weighted down by water soaking their feathers. The guys that come along just for the poker and boozing began to appreciate being cooped up.

Margaret came around to tell me Bertha said we'd ought to have a fire in the furnace to take off the chill.

"So why didn't she have you tell Hank that?"

She smiled. "She says he'd make it too rambunctious. It needs your delicate touch."

That wasn't Bertha's style at all. I guessed Margaret was using her own system for handling things smoothly and of course went for it. Since it was only October I just fired up the furnace under the lobby, which is a hot air job. I figured if people were up in their rooms in the west wing they could pile on blankets.

At noon Syvertson took off for lunch and Joey shambled into the lobby. Margaret came behind him and asked if he'd like lunch in the kitchen? Bertha was making cold pork sandwiches. Joey's gloomy face brightened and a few minutes later Hank, Joey and I were sitting in the booth by the kitchen, feeding our faces.

I asked Joey how it was going.

"Mostly no place. I know there was some nastiness at the beer parlor last night when Abe went to fetch his wife, but there wasn't a fight or even an argument. Abe just latched on to Florine and brought her back."

"What was she doing when Abe got there?"

"She was in a booth with Pat Bertrand and Turner. Waterboy was there too, and Swede. Nobody heard anything last night or this morning in the hotel except Bull, who heard the shower first."

"You know if Turner ever met Bull's wife?" I asked.

Joey swallowed some sandwich and shook his head. "I never asked. She's not here, I didn't even think of her. You know something I don't?"

"Nope. Just a thought."

Joey smiled at Margaret when she came with coffee refills and when she had returned to the kitchen, he leaned toward me.

"Abe admitted he didn't sleep too fast last night. Says he heard two guys talking down by the front door pretty late. Sounded like you and Turner."

I said he was right and told about our walk and talk.

He leaned back. "You think he was going tomcatting?"

"Yup. He was pretty interested in his watch."

"He had a date with the letter writer."

I nodded and lifted my head as I heard the front door open in the lobby. There was some murmuring and then Doc Feeney padded into the dining room and up to our booth. He stopped beside Joey and held out his fist.

Joey spread his big paw and Doc dropped a shiny steel ball into his palm. It was the size of a marble shooter, what kids call a steely.

"This what did it?" asked Joey.

"It had a strong influence."

"Go deep?"

"Deep enough to kill."

"A slingshot," I said.

They both looked at me doubtfully.

"It would've been at point-blank range. That'd penetrate."

Neither of them liked the idea much but couldn't improve on it. Joey tried to get a commitment from Doc about the angle and Doc shook that off. You couldn't assume any particular angle on a man giving himself a shower.

Margaret came in to offer Doc coffee but he turned it down and left.

Joey slumped back in the booth and stared gloomily across the dining room.

"This sure's hell doesn't get us any closer to knowing who done it."

SEVEN

After lunch I went to buy tobacco and left Joey sitting in the dining room scowling at the list of people he'd talked to so far. He looked about as happy as a man full of bean gas sitting at a church funeral.

Waterboy ran the newsstand and tobacco shop on Main across from Eric's Cafe´. I found him parked on a stool thumbing through a new *Saturday Evening Post* while chewing on a Mars bar.

He took my nickel for a sack of Bull Durham and watched me roll my smoke. His baby face was almost sullen. He looked like a stranger.

"Did Turner ever unload on you?" I asked.

"About what?"

"Anything."

"What're you after?"

"Whoever killed him. I don't know what'll help so I got to fish till I get a nibble. Last night I took a walk with him. He talked a lot and when we came back to the hotel he didn't go to his room, he headed south and was looking at his watch. I think he had a date."

47

Waterboy's cherub mouth softened into a grin. "That's my boy."

"When Joey and I went through his stuff we found a letter from a girl. It wasn't signed, dated or anything but we figure it was from somebody in town and we know it said Turner'd telephoned her before coming. You got any notion who it might've been?"

He looked suspicious again. "What difference does it make? He was killed in the hotel shower. Or you think he was killed south and carried back?"

"Not likely. But if we knew who the girl was, we might know who was jealous or some other goofy connection might show. He tell you anybody he'd been in touch with around here?"

"He kept in touch with lots, you can bet on that. Turner wasn't a guy who'd ever let a girl go that he'd ever liked or had."

"He didn't love 'em and leave 'em?"

"Oh, he left 'em all right, but he never forgot a one and he always hoped to come back for more."

"He ever go with Rose?"

"Everybody's gone with Rose."

"It was nothing special?"

"They were all special to Turner. He never screwed a girl he didn't love—and he loved 'em all."

"You know how he's been making his living the last few years?"

"If he got paid for screwing, he'd been a millionaire. He told most people, like Bull, he was doing insurance but he wasn't. Sold clothes awhile, did some stemming. You know what that is?"

I admitted my ignorance, which pleased him.

"That's guys that hang around the main street in places like Minneapolis, on what they call the main stem. Stop girls and sign them up for appointments and then go around to their apartments and pitch pots and pans or dishes. You can make money and get laid like crazy. At least *he* could. But he didn't really like it much. I mean the selling. Getting laid he liked fine. The last I heard he'd been working for some bootleggers. That was just before Roosevelt killed the moonshine business with repeal. Told me he even got shot at once. But I don't know what he'd been doing lately. Didn't have a chance for a real talk."

His voice got thick and he blinked off a couple tears.

He wouldn't tell me anything special about particular girls Turner'd romanced in school, kept insisting he played them all equal. The talking got him so depressed he finally told me it'd be nice if I'd just leave him alone and I did.

I tried Eric's Café, looking for Rose but she was out. Eric gave me a long sad story about women and their female troubles and was telling me more than I wanted to hear about his mother before I broke it off and moved on.

Rose lived in a small white house well back from the street about three blocks south of the hotel. The rain had let up by the time I headed that way but drippings from the box elders and elms kept plopping on my head and shoulders as I hiked the sidewalk. She came to the door wearing a blue robe and scuff slippers. Her dark hair was tangled and she had that beat look women get from crying.

"I'd have brought you flowers," I said, "but there were none growing along the way."

She tried a smile that didn't come off and said I always was a thoughtful fellow and the biggest favor I could do right now was to leave her alone.

"You heard about Turner?"

She nodded and her eyes began to water.

"Let me talk to you."

"You don't want to talk to me, you want me to do the talking, isn't that it?"

"Yeah."

"How come you didn't bring a bottle? That's what you always did when you went up to question Lil."

"You know too much about me, but you're no Lil. Come on, Rose, let me in."

She sighed, pushed the door a little and let me pull it wide enough to slip by. I waited until she started off and followed her into the shadowy house.

We sat in her small living room. The shades were drawn and it was so dark I could just make out the shapes of chairs and the couch and see she had a deep red carpet that barely filled the room's center. There were small pictures on the walls. I recognized the Lone Wolf and a shot of Inspiration Falls from Yellowstone, both pictures you'd find in half the Corden homes.

"Did Turner have a date with you last night?" I asked.

"You working for Joey?"

"In a way. Not official. You don't have to tell me anything."

She touched her hair, suddenly got up and walked out, saying she'd be right back. I listened to her run up the stairs, wondering what the hell, and then she was back carrying a hair brush. She sat down and began running it through her hair in slow, careful strokes, tilting her head to one side and then the other.

"Did you like Harmon?" she asked.

It took a second for me to remember that was Turner's first name. When I got it, I nodded and said yes. The admission surprised me. "We took a walk last night and talked some. I got the feeling he'd been better off if he'd just died when the last football season ended."

"He was the saddest boy I ever knew," she said.

I watched her brushing her hair. It crackled.

"We found your letter in his suitcase," I said. "You promised to see him if he'd write to you. Did he?"

"Why'd you think it was my letter?" she asked, still brushing.

"The handwriting and the style."

She smiled sadly. "You shouldn't lie to me, Carl. You've never seen my writing and we both know that letter wasn't signed. Why'd you try to trick me?"

"I'm sorry, Rose. I get so used to people lying to me when I ask about murder I just forget everybody's not the same. Did he answer your letter?"

She lowered the brush to her lap, shook her head so the hair rippled and finally nodded.

"It was a nice letter. He said he wanted to talk to me. That I was the most understanding girl he'd ever known." She made a wry mouth. "It was his line that always worked. He said he'd come by here around one or so and please wait for him and of course I did and he stayed until nearly dawn. We didn't talk much. He went to sleep after and then I woke him and told him he had to get back to the hotel before light and he went. I thought I'd probably never see him again but I didn't dream it'd be impossible."

She put her head down and cried so softly I could only hear her breath but her shoulders heaved.

"He tell you anything about what he was doing?" I asked when she straightened up a little and wiped her face with a hanky taken from her robe pocket. She shook her head, rose and walked into the kitchen. After a couple seconds she appeared in the door and asked if I'd like coffee. I said yes and she disappeared. I heard water running, then the puff of a gas jet being lit.

She came and leaned against the door jamb.

"Harmon never could decide what to do. For a living, I mean. He always thought somebody'd come around and say, 'Hey, Heart, I've got just the job for you' and suddenly he'd be on easy street. The last thing he told me was some fellow had asked him to be a union organizer. He said he was thinking about it. He liked talking to people. Of course there'd be more to it than talking. He didn't tell me what but I figured him being very strong and quick might be a big help in that business."

My face must've given me away because she started nodding. "Oh yes, he could be tough. He was real proud of breaking a fellow's arm in one of their games. That's a side he didn't show many but he told me all about it. I bet he told me more than anybody else."

"You go with him a lot?"

She looked away from me and I guessed she was trying to decide how much she wanted to admit.

"No," she said at last. "He only came to me when things went wrong. The first time was when they lost a game his junior year. He fumbled the ball and the other team won and he felt so awful I was sorry for him and the next thing I knew I'd sort of comforted him right into my bed. He thought I was something wonderful then. Later he came to me when things didn't go right with other girls. He never admitted that right out but he'd always talk about how I wasn't like the others and I'd be wonderful for a night."

"From all I heard, I thought he never missed with one he wanted."

"They all miss sometime. Even Harmon Turner. He had to have them all, even ones that belonged to his friends. Like he never cared really about Florine, but she was teasy and married to another tough guy and that was irresistible to poor Harmon."

"You know Abe Parker very well?"

"As well as most of them. He'd have tried to beat up on Harmon if he caught them together, but he'd never sneak around and kill him. Abe's just not that kind of fella."

I watched her, trying to figure how a woman so good and kind could always wind up with losers. She turned away from my gaze and moved back into the kitchen. A few seconds later she returned with two cups of coffee, handed me one and settled on the sofa across from me, carefully tucking her robe around her legs.

"I look a wreck," she said. "Feel like one. I don't want to talk anymore, Carl. I'm too dumb to tell you anything anyway. Talk to me, will you?"

"What can I tell you you want to hear? That you were the best thing that ever happened to Turner or Buff?"

Buff was another of her lovers who'd died young.

"I wish I could believe that," she said.

"You can. The only trouble is, neither one of them had brains enough to figure it out for themselves. You've been wasted."

She straightened up, gave me a hard look and said, "I suppose I should've saved myself for you?"

"Well, at least you'd have wound up with a survivor. But no, you could do lots better. Still can. You're not exactly ancient and you're a hell of a woman."

"Oh sure." She sipped the coffee and cradled the cup with both hands. They were big and red. She wore no rings.

"Why'd your wife leave you?" she asked.

"Because the Wilcox Hotel wasn't the Ritz."

She frowned.

"I lied to her," I confessed. "Made the place sound a lot bigger than it was. Or maybe I remembered it better when I told her about it. The place shrank when I was gone. And anyway, she was a woman that swallowed everything so big that I couldn't resist handing her whoppers. At least I couldn't then. She wanted to be rich and famous. You know she played a banjo?"

Rose shook her head.

"She did. Not bad either. Played in vaudeville in towns around New York."

"How'd she happen to marry you?"

"I made her laugh when she needed a few. What it really came down to was, she'd had a tough time with a couple pretty boys and she got a notion that a homely guy'd be more loving and, you know, grateful. Pearl was a girl that got ideas and lived by them."

"Did you love her?"

"I think I did when she played the banjo. And when we were loving. It might've worked if she hadn't talked so much. She wanted me to do rope tricks on the stage with her."

"I bet you'd have been good."

"I'd have felt like an organ grinder's monkey. Wouldn't do it. That made her mad. She figured everybody'd ought to want being on stage, that's all that counted for her. Being on stage. The hell with it."

"But you'd have been able to travel and maybe made a lot of money—"

I didn't bother to disillusion her about how much money third-rate vaudevillians got or how crumby that kind of travel is.

We talked some more and when I figured she'd cheered up a little I told her thanks for the talk and coffee and she said it was nothing and I went.

Time was when I'd have parlayed that visit into bed but I didn't have the heart to take advantage of her weak moment and felt sure she'd be upset about it afterward.

I always liked Rose.

EIGHT

I found Hank in the lobby sticking lettuce between the narrow bars of Gabriel's cage. The canary was skittering around inside, peeping furiously.

"How's Joey doing with the third degree?" I asked.

"Nobody's broken down and confessed yet."

"Who's he talked to?"

"Everybody and then some. He worked on Margaret and even Bertha."

"I hope he kept her away from her cleaver."

"She was pretty docile."

I didn't ask him where he got that word; noticing his vocabulary only encouraged him. And I couldn't believe the word had anything to do with our mad cook.

I went over to the dining room and looked in. Joey was sitting with his back to the kitchen in the booth nearest the swinging door. The mayor was beside him. I couldn't see who faced them.

I went back to Hank and asked where everybody was.

"Most of them are up in their rooms. Napping, I'd guess. I don't think many got much sleep last night. A few never came back from lunch."

I strolled back to the kitchen through the dining room. The mayor looked up but was so preoccupied he didn't seem to recognize me. He looked back at Doug Otte, who didn't notice me either.

Margaret sat at the table beside the windows overlooking the back lot, where clotheslines were still stretched above the gravelly yard. She'd been sewing a button on a white blouse and glanced up at me with a questioning look when I moved onto the chair across from her.

"Hank says Joey gave you the third degree," I said.

"He asked if I'd heard anything," she said as she knotted her job and cut the thread.

"From the kitchen I doubt you'd heard a shotgun blast up in the shower."

"We didn't."

"You make any early calls?"

"Hank made them. He didn't hear anything either—except the shower running early."

I didn't ask where Bertha was. She took a two-hour nap every afternoon. When you haul around nearly three hundred pounds at high speed starting a little after four in the morning, by noon you need rest.

"You ever meet Turner?" I asked.

She leaned back and folded her arms under her small breasts. "Joey asked that too. How could I have met him? I don't come from Corden and I've never been in the Cities."

"Yeah, well, he seems to have met most women in the territory. I just wondered."

"I hear you killed a man in Toqueville. With a cornstalk. Is that true?"

"No."

"You didn't kill him?"

"Oh yeah. But it wasn't in Toqueville, it was on a farm about five miles south of town. And I didn't do it with a cornstalk, it was mostly the kicking did it."

"Because he killed a little girl, is that right?"

"I didn't know he'd killed her yet. But I knew he might and he'd already killed a couple guys."

"How'd you feel about it?"

"Pretty good. It beat letting him chop me up with the hoe he'd brought along."

She shuddered and smoothed out the blouse she'd been working on.

"You don't want to believe everything Bertha tells you," I said. "She never gets out of the hotel. All she knows is what she gets told."

She gave me a short smile. "Bertha doesn't miss much. And she thinks the world of your parents."

I thought of saying that should tell her a hell of a lot about Bertha but kept it in and went over to check the big coffee pot on the range. It was hot and I poured a cup for me after she turned down my offer to her.

I sat down again.

"Ma says you're a widow. Got any kids?"

She leaned both elbows on the table, pushed her glasses up on her nose and regarded me soberly. "Just one."

"Boy or girl?"

"Girl."

"Where is she?"

"Far away."

"California?"

She nodded.

"They all wind up in California or the Cities, don't they? She must be pretty young."

"That's how she seems to me. I had her a long time ago, when *I* was very young. Actually, right now she's older than I was when she was born."

I looked at her hands, which rested on the white blouse and guessed she was forty or so. She had long, tapered fingers and neat, unpainted nails.

"I'm forty-two," she said.

"What happened to your husband?"

"We broke up. I'm not going to talk about that."

"What'd you do when that happened?"

"Lived with my parents, took care of them till they died a year ago. Unlike me, my mother bore her daughter late. The one advantage of having children late is that they tend to take care of their parents."

"That's only the parents' advantage."

"I considered it a privilege," she said with a mocking smile and I found myself staring at her mouth too long. She turned and looked into the yard where a gusting wind ruffled but couldn't lift the sodden leaves. Rain was falling steadily again.

"I don't envy the hunters," she said, then looked at me once more. "You're kind of a hunter, aren't you?"

"Depends on what you mean."

"You hunt killers."

That seemed a weird notion but I couldn't find a way to deny it.

"How many've you caught?" she asked.

"Well, I haven't got a gun so there's no place to put the notches. Not many. Lots of times it hasn't been too clear-cut."

"I saw a book of poetry in your room," she said. "Moore."

"Yeah. Ma gave it to me."

"Have you read it?"

"Some. He's sort of third-rate Omar Khayyam."

"Or Edward Fitzgerald." Her smile was still mocking. I wondered if she'd feel bony in bed.

"I suspect," she said, "that if you were to investigate this murder, it'd have a much better chance of being solved than with Joey working on it."

"Don't let him hear that. He's already uncomfortable about me."

"It's not that I think he's stupid, I'm sure he's a fine policeman for Corden, but he's short on imagination. I hear you have a great deal of that."

"I guess you've heard it's mostly misapplied."

"Oh yes. Without you, people in Corden would have little to talk about."

There was a stirring upstairs, which meant Bertha was either rolling over or getting up from her beauty sleep. Margaret pushed her chair back, stood and carefully folded the blouse.

"We'll be starting supper soon, I'm going to put this away."

I guessed she didn't want Bertha to find her sitting cozily with me in the kitchen and began to understand why this woman had kept our cook pacified. She knew instinctively that nothing'd make Bertha madder than somebody being friendly with me in her kitchen.

I watched Margaret go to the stairway door, open it and start up the angled steps. Her hips didn't look a bit bony and they moved beautifully. With a sigh I headed back out to the lobby.

Hank intercepted me in the hall and edged me into Ma's private dining room off the main one.

"Can we rent out ten yet?" he asked.

"Sure. Joey's been all through it."

"Two guys are asking for it. They heard about the murder and figured there'd be space."

That sounded like a sweet pair of vultures but I couldn't think of any reason to turn them down and walked back with Hank to the register counter.

The taller of the two guys had a built-in worried look which turned near desperate when I told him the room would cost six bucks or twenty-five for the week. He looked at his partner, who looked like nothing in this world had ever worried him. His grin was wide enough to dimple his earlobes.

"We'll take it for a week," he said. "Where'd the guy croak?"

"In the shower."

"Fine," said the smiley one, looking at his partner. "You got nothing to worry about."

I turned the register their way and the smiler signed his name, Darrell Gustafson. The worrier's scribble was so bad I couldn't read it and asked him what it was.

"Downer," he said. "Wilfred W."

I said fine and Hank led them upstairs. I noticed they came from Iowa according to the register and tried to remember where I'd heard the town name before but couldn't place it.

Before Hank returned, Florine sailed down the steps and swished into the lobby looking decked out for high tea with the Queen of England.

"I see somebody's taking ten. How'd they know about the vacancy?"

"I think the word's out. We haven't had any other murders this week."

She caught and didn't appreciate the irony. "You're rather used to murders, aren't you?"

"I don't think I'll ever get used to them."

She turned away and looked over toward the Playhouse across the street. "Will there be a dance there tonight?"

"Yup."

"I don't suppose the band'll be much."

"Well, Guy Lombardo couldn't make it but the one they got can keep time."

"By the clock or the beat?"

"Both. They have to know when to quit because the law says midnight is pumpkin time."

"I suppose I'll have to be at their dumb old reunion."

She said that with a pout that was supposed to be sexy and it worked pretty good.

"Maybe it'll break up early," I said.

Before she could react Hank came down and gave her his wide-eyed admiring look. Her pout disappeared and turned into a wicked grin. "I'll bet you go to the dances."

"Sure," said Hank. "Every Saturday night."

"I bet you're a keen dancer."

"Only when I've got a good partner. Will you be there?"

I glanced at the stairs, thinking this'd be a lovely time for Abe to show.

"You want to check each other out," I said, "I can hum."

They both laughed but I wasn't in on it.

Pat's appearance broke up the budding romance and the two women set off to see the town in the rain. Before leaving they both smiled at Hank, who grinned hard enough to strain his jaw.

I let him know it wasn't smart to flirt with married women and he waved me off, saying they were way too old for him and I said that was right, they'd eat him alive and from his expression I could tell the idea tickled him pink so I dropped it.

The room two crowd drifted in early in the afternoon, wet, cold and about half proud since three of the five had made kills and two got three apiece. Kinman, who was the oldest and had the biggest mouth, let me know how sharp they were and asked if the butcher still dressed and packed birds for hunters. I said he did. They were still milling around in the lobby when Joey popped in from the dining room wanting to know if these were the dudes who'd gone hunting at dawn. When I confirmed that he told them to get into dry clothes and get down to the dining room, he wanted to question them. I could see Kinman bristle at his tone but when he learned what it was all about he cooled quick and led his gang up to change.

Joey stared after them a moment, then sat down on the rocker beside the register and gave a big sigh.

"Not getting anywhere?" I asked.

He shook his head and glanced at Hank. "When'd you make your first call?"

"Quarter to five. There was no light in the shower and nobody in the halls. Not a sound till I knocked on two."

"Get an answer quick?"

"Yeah. Guy hollered okay right off."

"Think he was already up?"

"I didn't see any light through the transom."

"There's something damned screwy here," Joey told me. "Why'd they get up so damned early they couldn't get a cup of coffee and go barreling out to hunt when you couldn't see a thing in the sky, let alone on the ground?"

"Some guys just have to do anything that's against the law."

He considered that with some gravity and had the good grace not to make some crack about me being an expert in that line.

I asked him what'd happened to our mayor.

"Went over to City Hall or home, I don't know or care."

"Maybe *he* had something against Turner. Know if the mayor's wife ever met our football hero?"

"No I don't, but if he had he wouldn't't've given her a glance and if he had, can you think of anybody unlikelier than Syvertson standing on a bureau at five in the morning, shooting a slingshot over a partition at a naked man in a shower?"

"I try to keep an open mind. Maybe his wife did it because Turner didn't give her the eye or anything more penetrating."

He gave me a baleful look and got to his feet as the men from room two came straggling down the stairs. Kinman, still in the leader role, stopped in front of Joey. He was a solid man with a forehead on its way to the nape of his neck and a jaw like a snowplow blade. All his hair seemed to have wound up in bushy eyebrows that stood out like awnings over his dark, glowering eyes.

"I'll start with you," said Joey. "The others wait here in the lobby. Carl, come along."

We went through the dining room to the booth by the kitchen door and Joey waved Kinman into the seat facing the distant east windows. We slid in across from him.

"So," said Joey. "You're from Detroit?"

"That's what I wrote on the register."

"What do you do for a living?"

"Run a hardware store."

Joey's gloom lightened. "That right? My favorite kind of store. Who runs it when you're hunting?"

"My oldest son."

Joey liked that too. He almost smiled. A family hardware store. Kinman's snowplow jaw relaxed some and he took on an expression more smug than belligerent.

"Why'd you guys get up so early?" I asked.

"To go hunting," he said without looking my way.

"In the dark?"

He still didn't look at me but the smug expression left. "We had a ways to drive."

"Where?"

"West of Dunlap." He sat back in the booth, glanced at me, then faced Joey again.

"If you left around five you had two hours before daylight. You could go eighty to a hundred miles in that time. Dunlap's only thirty."

"We stopped for breakfast."

"Where'd you find breakfast before seven?"

"Know a farmer out that way. His wife fed us."

"Who's that?"

"Nobody you know."

"I know just about everybody within driving distance inside an hour. Ones I don't, Joey does. Try us."

"Name's Olson."

"We got lots of them. Which one?"

"Ole."

"Come on, man, half the Olsons're called that."

"James, goddamn T. Olson."

"Fine, there's a different name: James goddamn T. Olson. I admit I don't know him. How about you, Joey?"

Joey shook his head. The charm of the hardware family was lost. He stared at Kinman with the sad disapproval he's given me over the years.

Kinman was scowling at me by then and it was so fierce his eyebrows made a V down to his nose.

"What the hell's it to you where we had breakfast?" he asked
me.

"We want to know where the hell you were when a man got
murdered upstairs. Nothing important. Just murder. Your cock-
and-bull story of going to a farmer's place before dawn on the
way to hunt pheasants before daylight stinks, but I'm willing to
be convinced and Joey already figures you must be okay because
you run, or say you do, a hardware store. You've never been here
before, have you?"

"Yeah, I have. Four years ago. You were probably in prison
then. I didn't see you around."

"Great. You're one up on me. So tell us where this James
goddamn T. Olson's farm is."

"It's got nothing to do with anything you need to know. All
you got to do is ask my friends out there if I was murdering
anybody this morning. We were together all the time and we
didn't kill anybody in a party either. There's no way in hell
you're gonna stick me or all of us with any murder in this crumby
hotel."

Of course he was right. His four stooges agreed they'd stopped
at a farm for breakfast but couldn't tell us where it was or who
owned it. The only thing they were certain of was they'd never
split up for any appreciable time. Joey managed to make each one
admit he'd not kept Kinman company when he went to the
outhouse at the farm or to the toilet in the hotel. None of them
admitted hearing the shower running.

I asked where they'd stayed when they hunted the years they
didn't stay in Corden. Only one guy told us he'd been with
Kinman before. He said they'd stayed in the Lowery Hotel in
Aquatown, which had burned down last New Year's Eve.

Joey gave up on them finally after making sure they planned to
stick around for the rest of their hunting time. When they were
gone we sat in the booth awhile, talking them over. I didn't really
believe any of them had done in Turner but their obvious

covering for Kinman convinced us both they were up to something foul and we couldn't just forget about it.

"Well hell," said Joey at last. "I'm gonna go get supper and forget it awhile. See you later."

NINE

Most of the hunters were back by the time I got into the lobby
and looked out on the heavy mist fogging streetlights down Main.
Hank sat in a rocker glowering at the floor he'd mopped shiny
that morning, which had been trampled by muddy boots the past
couple hours. He didn't cheer up any when I suggested he add a
little manure and make it rich for spring planting.

Gustafson, the smiler from Iowa, kept hanging around and I
noticed him edging toward the dining room door.

"You get supper downtown," I told him. "The dining room's
closed."

He said yeah, he knew that, just looking around. His grin
galled me more than was reasonable but I managed to keep from
telling him the hotel had private places and he damned well better
look around elsewhere. He stared past me, hitched up his slack
pants and drifted back beside his partner, Downer, who was
rubbernecking at newspapers on the table under the wall clock.

I parked in Elihu's chair as Phil Jacobson and Doug Otte came
down and asked if Abe or Muggsy had gone out already. I said
no, they were probably waiting around for their wives, who'd be
gussying up for the party.

Phil's thick, dark hair had been tamed some by brushing or hair oil and he was wearing a dark gray suit and shined oxfords. He looked out at his Olds and then at Turner's gleaming LaSalle and the corners of his mouth drooped. Otte sat gingerly in a rocker facing me and shook his head.

"I really owe you, Wilcox," he said, but the soreness was too much to make him sound ready to collect.

Phil sat beside him and asked if it was true I was the last guy to talk with Turner.

"I guess so, unless the guy that planted the steely in his head had something to say."

"What a waste," said Phil. "He had everything going for him if he'd just used it right."

Otte snorted. "What he had going for him he used too much. That was his trouble. He was bound to either screw himself to death or get killed by some bimbo's partner."

Phil ignored that and frowned at me.

"What'd he talk to you about?"

"Nothing special."

"He didn't say anything about his old buddies and old times?"

"He seemed to think they were all great."

I could see he was fishing and sensed that he knew I did but couldn't help pushing.

"Old Turner," he said, "just had to keep swiping other guys' women. It got so we were all doing that. Like he said, competition was what made us go."

"Nobody was into it like Turner," said Otte.

"He move in on both you guys?" I asked.

"He did on Phil," said Otte.

"Yeah? How about you and that Comfrey chick?" demanded Phil.

"I never got anyplace with her."

"You sure tried. He cut you out quick."

"No quicker'n he took Bunny from you."

"Oh well," said Phil casually, "anybody could take Bunny anytime."

"Who was Bunny?" I asked.

"Coach's kid. Bunny Titus," said Otte. "We called her Bunny rabbit."

"Fast, huh?" I said.

"That was just talk," said Phil, getting up. "Come on, Doug, let's get a beer."

I watched them walking east, Phil Jacobson, tall and still slim, Otte wide and hunched a little, walking carefully like a kid with a wad in his pants.

Bertha served the hotel crew meat loaf with creamed potatoes, cooked carrots and peas and topped it off with fresh brownies. The dessert was for Hank's benefit because he preferred them to the devil's food cake with fudge frosting that Elihu and I favored. Devil's food was the only thing I knew of that Elihu and I ever had in common.

Bertha ate with Hank and then Hank watched the lobby while I ate with Margaret.

"Where'd you live in Iowa?" I asked Margaret.

"Colstrom."

"Where's that from Indigo?"

She thought about that some and said she guessed south and a little east. No, she'd not been there. She'd never traveled much of anywhere except for two years in Aberdeen where she'd gone to teacher's college. After that she'd taught primary grades in Colstrom's school. It turned out she only did that one year because her father became ill and she was needed full-time at home.

She watched me while she talked. Her lively eyes went over my face and hands, looking as if they were expecting to find something that'd make her laugh. Her life sounded like an old maid's but there wasn't a suggestion of a dried-up woman in her tone or manner.

"Where'd you meet your husband?" I asked.

"Church. He sat in front of me one Sunday and while walking out said I had a lovely voice for hymns and things rather went from there."

"You got married while your folks were still living?"

She looked down at the remnant of her meat loaf for a split second and then up again. "Yes. It was very difficult. We lived next door to them and I kept helping out and my husband was very understanding at first but after the baby things turned hectic. He felt I neglected him and my baby and pretty soon it was obvious things couldn't be worked out. He took a job in another town and eventually we were divorced."

She said all this as if she were talking about strangers. Then her neutral expression turned sad. "The divorce shocked my father. I think it killed him. Mother died within six months and all of a sudden I was free to take care of a husband but then I didn't have one anymore."

She straightened up and smiled. "I'm not the self-pitying kind. Now it just all seems ironic. The truth is, I wouldn't have been terribly happy living with my husband. He was not affectionate."

I asked what he did.

"Taught at the high school."

"What?"

"Oh, algebra, some history. A little physical ed."

I asked where he was now and she looked uninterested and said she'd no idea.

While we were eating brownies I asked if Ma had warned her against me.

Her fine teeth gleamed as she tilted her head back in a laugh. "Oh yes. She said you'd a great weakness for widows in particular and women in general and you weren't to be trusted an inch."

"I told her the same thing," announced Bertha from her counter.

"Don't pay her any attention," I told Margaret. "She's just jealous. I don't know how to account for Ma's prejudice."

"Well," said Margaret, "if liking widows is a weakness, I think it's a nice one."

She got up and cleared the table after that. Bertha moved around like a sullen hippo and glowered me out of the kitchen.

As I shoved through the swinging door to the dining room I met Gustafson's ear-to-ear grin. We both pulled up.

"I was wondering could I put in a order for lunches tomorrow?" he asked as the door closed behind me.

"You want cold pork, cold beef or peanut butter and jelly?"

"Well, I'd like to talk with the gal that does 'em— "

"Nobody talks to Bertha in her kitchen but family and even they have special hours for the privilege. You tell me what you want, I'll see you get it."

"Well, me and Will'd like one of each. I hear she's got a salad dressing special for peanut butter and jelly—"

"You want it, you got it. Got a thermos?"

He did and we made arrangements while I herded him back toward the lobby. I watched him leave with his solemn buddy and asked Hank how come he'd let that bastard slip past him.

Hank said he must've snuck down the hall behind the counter when Will Downer was buying cigars and gabbing.

"Old gloomy was gabbing? What about?"

"He'd heard about the reunion party tonight and asked what it was all about. Wanted to know how many of the people staying in the hotel'd be going."

I told him to go eat and he didn't object.

Abe, Florine, Pat and Muggsy came down and paraded through the lobby. The ladies were done up like Mrs. Astor's horse and even their men looked pretty respectable in dark suits, white shirts and dead ties. Abe had shined his shoes.

They didn't pause to pass the time of day but sashayed out and headed for Eric's Café. It was beginning to look like Turner's death wasn't putting much of a damper on the evening plans. That made me wonder about the real feelings of this gang toward their old buddy.

Bull Dickey came down before they were out of sight and, after a glance around, wandered near Gabriel's cage and asked when he sang.

"He doesn't have a schedule," I said. "I guess he prefers mornings most."

"How do you know it's a male?"

"I don't *know*. But Elihu says only the males sing and God knows Gabe sings. How do you think this reunion thing's going to come off?"

He cocked his broad head. "Because of Turner? I think it'll put a damper on things till a few folks get enough to drink, then they'll get talkative and later loud and finally maudlin."

"I guess you don't expect to enjoy it much."

He sat in a rocker and said he guessed it'd be okay.

"What do you do for a living these days?" I asked.

He took a stubby pipe from his coat pocket and started stoking it up. "What'd you guess?"

"No notion."

He smiled, tamped the tobacco down with a little metal gadget and said, "I teach history at the University of Minnesota, European and Greek." He grinned at my reaction and said he would imagine I thought he'd be a professional wrestler or maybe a bouncer.

"No. Coach told me you were the smartest guy on the team. I thought you'd probably be in something like insurance."

"Yeah, well, that's what football players are supposed to do, live off the alumni. I don't know where I went wrong but mostly blame it on a history prof who hooked me on his field. I didn't have time to keep up class work but he liked questions I asked and needled me about being a Neanderthal man. It got to me. In my junior year I decided to drop football and get an education. But my sponsor talked me into staying by saying he'd guarantee my tuition after my four years on the team. He kept his word."

"He get you the teaching job too?"

"He didn't hurt any, but I was qualified by then. I'm working on a doctorate now and figure on tenure in a few years."

I didn't know what the hell tenure was but he made it sound like he had things sandbagged so I figured it was good.

Ed Folsum joined us then but didn't sit down. He'd played fullback for Corden High and had been tough and eager. He ran low with his shoulders so far ahead of his hips that the best way to stop him was get out of the way and let him fall on his face. The kids playing against him never learned that and kept him up by getting in his way. His face was getting jowly and his belly round. I'd heard Otte kidding him earlier, saying he looked pregnant. Ed answered it was no wonder, he'd sure been fucked around enough. He worked for a plumbing contractor in St. Paul and obviously didn't miss any meals.

Bull got up with some signs of reluctance and went off with Ed. Then Hank said if I didn't mind he was going to the bathroom and then change clothes for the dance later on. I didn't mind.

I'd rolled a couple smokes and watched a lot of Model T's come into town with a few Chevies and even a Model A or two when I heard a light step behind me and turned to see Margaret glancing over the register.

"Recognize any names?" I asked.

She lifted her dark eyes and shook her head. She was wearing a navy blue dress with a white collar and looked trim and fresh as a schoolgirl. I asked if she were going to the dance.

"Think I'd get asked if I did?"

"Seems more than likely."

She sat down, crossed her ankles and touched the hair bun on the back of her neck with both hands. That pulled the dress close and showed her neat, small breasts. She caught my glance and lowered her arms.

"What did you do in the Philippines?" she asked.

"Helped fortify Corregidor the first half, beachcombed the second."

"The beachcombing came after you were discharged, right? After you kicked an MP?"

"I kicked the MP in France. Actually it was in the tail but it happened in France. He was leaning over a canal side and it seemed the natural thing to do. In the Philippines it was for insubordination. Against a superior officer. I didn't think he was that superior."

She laughed and shook her head.

We both heard steps coming down the stairs and she made a move to rise, then thought better of it and settled back as Smiley Gustafson and Downer walked into the lobby. Gustafson's grin disappeared a second before returning all wet with a swab from his dog tongue.

"Well," he said, "as I live and breathe, if it isn't Miz Margaret."

"Hello, Gus."

He stopped in front of her. "I heard you was around but was beginning to wonder if they'd locked you up in the cellar. You're lookin' good."

She said thanks without enthusiasm.

"Me and Will're going over town, have a beer. Wanta come along and kick around old times?"

"No, thank you."

"Aw, come on. After a few snorts we'll go over to the dance hall. You like to dance—"

"I have other plans for the evening," she said in a voice that'd frost a torch.

"Come on, Margy—"

"She said no," I told him. "Go peel a peach."

He glanced around at me, looked up at his partner, then back at me.

"I suppose you got plans, huh?"

"Not yet."

He turned around to face me square. "I tell you what, shorty, you'd best stay out of my way."

"You want to dance," I said, getting up, "let's go outside and give it a whirl."

His grin was full again. I don't think a crocodile could show more teeth. I went out the door and he came close behind. I let him start to lift his hands and hit him. He slammed into the hotel wall, fell forward and caught my best hook, which sent him wheeling into his friend, who kept him from hitting the sidewalk too hard.

"The trouble with your friend," I told Will, "is he doesn't know how to take no for an answer."

"He can't help it," said Will mournfully, "that woman's put a spell on him. Makes him crazy."

Gus tried lifting his head but lost interest and settled down as if for a nap.

"How long's he known Margaret?" I asked.

"Oh, quite a while. Since before she lost her kid, ten years, maybe more."

"He the father?"

He looked at the folks gathering near and muttered something I didn't catch. Before I could ask more Joey came galloping up and wanted to know what was going on. I told him Gus'd tripped leaving the hotel and banged his head on the sidewalk. The conversation opened Gus's eyes, which looked glazed but not too blank and he let Will and me pick him up and brush him off.

"You all right?" asked Joey, staring at the darkening bruise on his jaw.

Gus wagged his head slowly, decided it was still attached to his neck and nodded.

"You want Doc to look at your head?"

Gustafson said he was finer than a fairy's fart and a moment later he and Will wandered east toward the beer parlor.

"All right," said Joey as folks began drifting away, "what really happened? Why'd you hit him?"

"He made a pass at Margaret and didn't know when to quit."

"So you called him out?"

"You think I should've argued his case?"

We both looked at the hotel window and saw Margaret standing inside, watching.

"Well," said Joey, "you impressed her. That's what it was really all about, wasn't it?"

"Don't go turning sour just because you got a murder you can't handle," I told him.

He turned away from the window, looked down the crowded street and shifted his hat on his head a couple times. It wound up straight as ever. "We got to talk about that."

"What part?"

"I think I can maybe work the younger kid of Kinman's crowd from room two. Find out where that farm they went to is. Where they spent their time. There's something real funny there. It's like Kinman'd rather face a murder charge than tell where he was and why."

"He was messing with somebody's wife," I said. "I don't figure that's got anything to do with our murder."

"Okay, but we can't settle for that. Would you go talk to people wherever that farm is if I get it located?"

"And leave the hotel in the middle of hunting season?"

"You wouldn't have to be gone more'n a couple hours. Hank, Bertha and Margaret can handle things."

I made him work on me a little more before agreeing to do what I was all set to do right off. As soon as that was agreed on, he had another proposition.

He said Eric wanted somebody around to keep the reunion party under control and thought if Joey went he'd put a damper on things. If I was to do it, nobody'd expect me to be a wet blanket and yet they'd stay in line.

"All you got to remember," said Joey, "is you don't have to prove anything to these guys. They all know you're handy even if you didn't have time for games."

"I thought you had a regular deputy."

"Don't kid me. Tim's fine for helping direct traffic and getting drunks off the sidewalk but he's not the man for this job and you know it."

So I said okay again. He looked relieved but not a lot because he figured there was always a risk I'd get too involved in the celebrating and tank up with the worst of them. He had the good sense not to warn me against it.

TEN

I never understood why Eric couldn't sell liquor in his café but was allowed to peddle beer in the upstairs party hall. The subject just never got discussed. There was a covered stairway up the west side of his building and you could enter directly from the street so maybe that was supposed to make the difference. Only there was a door to it from the café too, and Eric's help went through that and up to deliver platters of grub directly from the kitchen without hiking around outside during blizzards and rainstorms.

Whatever the legal technicalities, the reunion party for the 1924 Corden High Tigers took place up there. The bar ran from the top of the stairs to the east end of the hall and it offered draft beer and mixes for the hip flasks and brown-papered quarts of whiskey. I wasn't around to prevent tippling or high spirits, my job was to keep the breakage down and the roughhousing tolerable.

The minute I walked in the joint Eric grabbed my arm and begged me to take over the bar. His regular helper had been in a car accident that afternoon and was still in the hospital at

Aquatown. Joey hadn't said anything about me not tending bar so I figured it was a good front for my job as peacemaker and took it on.

Nobody in the crowd seemed surprised and I did a steady business trading smartass cracks with nearly everybody that bought a beer or a bottle of mix. There were no obvious signs of grief around the room, even Waterboy seemed to be having fun as usual. Swede wasn't looking gay but Lutherans seldom do so that seemed natural.

When I refilled his beer mug he leaned over it a moment, scowling.

I asked how he was doing and got a shrug.

"You been married about ten years now, right? Got any kids?" I asked.

He said no and drank some beer.

"I don't suppose you ever got in on any of the wild parties the team had after games, huh?"

"What do you mean, wild parties?"

"I heard there was some drinking and fooling around with girls. You ever get in on any of that stuff?"

He looked away. "Naw. Had to work."

"But I suppose Waterboy told you about what happened."

"Me and Waterboy weren't buddies. Back then he figured I was just a farm hick."

"Now you're different?"

"Naw. He is."

He said that without a gleam of humor and I looked past him toward the crowd and saw Waterboy watching us from the Jacobson table. Jacobson was talking to him and Otte was watching us. Waterboy got up and came over to Swede's side.

"Hey, buddy," he said, putting his hand on Swede's shoulder, "come on back to the table. You can talk to Carl anytime but these guys aren't around every day."

Swede nodded but didn't move. I wondered if he were already drunk.

Waterboy leaned closer. "You okay?"

"Fine," said Swede. He licked his lips.

"He's not used to boozing," Waterboy told me. "Gets to him quick."

Jacobson rose from his table, came over and patted Swede on the back.

"We've been talking about you. The old reliable. Steady and strong. You never got any real credit but by God we'd never have made it without Swede. I guess you didn't make a mistake in the last three years we played."

"Everybody makes mistakes," said Swede darkly. "Old Turner, you, Doug, Abe. Everybody."

"Well," laughed Jacobson, "I sure's hell did, and God knows Otte did, but we got by because the guys we played against made even more."

He patted Swede again and looked at me.

"What made him so steady was, he never lost his temper or got all hopped up like the rest of us. Just kept his head."

"I got mad," said Swede.

"Well, you sure never let anybody know."

Swede pulled out his pocket watch, glanced at it and said he'd better be going. They gave him arguments he ignored and he moved toward the stairway with Waterboy close. Jacobson watched them with an expression between exasperation and worry.

Swede met Bull Dickey coming up with Ed Folsum and got stopped for a few seconds before continuing on his way. A moment later Bull and Ed were at the bar.

I drew beers for them and Bull asked if I'd had a lot of experience behind a bar.

"Nope, only on the other side."

Ed drifted off to prowl the tables where there were a few women from the class of '24. None of them I knew were still single but not all had their hubbies along and Ed was always hopeful.

"I hear there's a new hired girl at the hotel," said Bull.

"We don't call Margaret a hired girl. She's more like a hostess."

"Oh? How's Bertha dealing with that?"

"It was her idea."

That awed him speechless for a while but finally he asked how Joey was doing with his investigation.

"Well, he's pretty sure Bertha didn't do it."

He grinned and asked if we knew how it'd been done yet.

"Slingshot."

"Uh-huh. Figures. There were a lot of them around."

"You know any experts?"

"Quite a few. Including me. Jacobson, Waterboy, Otte, Ed. We used to have contests. Turner was damned good, but I guess he couldn't have managed suicide with one."

Coach Titus came up the stairs and after looking over the room came to join us. I asked if he wanted a beer, he nodded and reached for his billfold.

"Beer's part of the package," I told him. "No charge."

"Bad policy with this crowd. These guys'll get smashed just to be sure they get their money's worth."

"Swede already crapped out," I said.

"I saw him heading home. Looked pretty steady, but then, he always was. The dullest son of a bitch I ever knew, but dependable. I suppose that's what dependability comes down to. Dull."

He looked at Bull and shook his head. "So. Here's the professor, swilling beer with the common folk. You want to level with us, Bull, didn't they hire you to recruit for the football team?"

"I just have to give passing grades to athletes."

Titus grinned at him, showing wolfish teeth.

"What they should have at your school is a guy like Turner, teaching courses on how to get women. He'd have told them better you hit guys than books, women prefer animals."

I wondered if the coach was an expert with a slingshot. He tried to be the kidder but everything came out bitter.

"You should've stayed in coaching," Bull told him. "You made a mistake getting out when you did."

"It was time," said Titus. "I was king of the heap. There was no way to go but down. All my players graduated with you."

The thought made him gloomy and he said he guessed he'd ought to circulate and drifted off.

"What happened to him?" I asked Bull.

"His daughter died the spring after our last season. He never got over it."

"I don't remember him having a wife."

"She never lived here. He was widowed early, before moving to Corden. An old woman lived in and took care of the girl but could never handle her."

"What'd the daughter die of?"

He sighed, took a drink from his mug and leaned both elbows on the bar. "There's lots of stories. Nobody knows for sure because she left town that spring, maybe it was right after Christmas vacation, I'm not sure. Some say she was pregnant and died in childbirth down in Iowa. Others said it was an abortion gone bad."

"How old was she?"

"About sixteen, maybe seventeen."

"You know her?"

"I saw her around a lot, sure. She was crazy about football, hung around the practices and went along on our trips. We all knew her. Her name was Bonita but everybody called her Bunny."

"What'd Titus say she died of?"

"Flu."

"But nobody believed it, right?"

"Swede might have. He's dumb enough."

"You think Turner knocked her up?"

"Maybe."

He frowned and glanced over his shoulder. Titus was across the hall, talking with Abe Parker and Florine. Bull looked back at me.

"Titus wasn't even staying in the hotel the night of the murder," he said.

"The door's never locked."

Bull shook his head. "He wouldn't have done it. He always pretended we were morons, especially Turner, but he loved that kid like a son. Don't let anybody tell you different. And it went both ways."

"I heard the coach thought you were the special guy."

"He thought I was bright, but he loved any guy that did the job and Turner did it with flash and soul. Coach knew who made him look good and he never forgot it. Being the state's top coach meant more to him than anything else in his life, including his kid."

"Maybe it looked different after she died."

He finished his beer, set it down carefully and nodded.

"You may be right, but I still don't believe he'd do Turner in. Never."

It was nearly seven-thirty when Eric's crew set up the buffet and all the crowd moved in like vultures to pile up their plates with stewed chicken and dumplings, mashed potatoes, sweet potatoes, spinach and cooked carrots. For dessert Eric went the whole hog and gave them apple pie à la mode.

I sat with Eric at a little table near the bar and he watched happily as the mob shoveled down the groceries while telling him the chicken was rubbery, the dumplings lead and the spinach poisonous. Waterboy even claimed the carrots were undercooked but like everybody else he ate like he never expected another meal.

When everybody was stuffed, Bull Dickey came on as master of ceremonies. He set up his table podium while the guys made loud remarks and smiled out over them until the room got quiet. Then his broad face turned sober.

"Fourteen years ago," he began, "Corden had a football team of over fifty percent rookies. They were too small, too dumb and too scared to have any business putting on helmets and cleats and trotting out on a field to do anything but maybe dance around a maypole. And these kids under a coach who didn't know as much about a football as a hockey puck, went out on football fields eight times that fall and got pounded into the turf. People made fun of them, opponents laughed at them and their coach died every weekend. A few guys, the smart ones, quit. But the rest hung on and ten years ago this fall, they played eight straight winning games. The people cheered and the opponents never laughed and at the end of the last game the players carried their coach off the field on their shoulders and saw the tough old bastard cry."

The crowd murmured, there were a few laughs and few cheers.

"Another guy was carried off the field that day. A guy too small to carry the waterbucket right—"

Everybody howled and those near enough banged Waterboy's back while he grinned and lifted his clinched hands like a winning boxer.

"—and there was still another guy," continued Bull, "the one who carried the ball and, more than any of us, made it happen. He was carried by us too. And tomorrow six of us will carry him for the last time. He'll seem a lot heavier carried by six men than he was when two of us did it leaving the football field. You might say he carried us for four years, because in a way, he did. Don't ever forget that. Don't ever forget him."

The room fell silent as a funeral parlor and for a moment Bull stood with both hands on the podium sides and stared down. Then he raised his head.

"This isn't a wake. This isn't even a farewell party. We aren't kids anymore. What happened ten years ago was something fine and fun, but it was ten years ago and we've got other things to do and think about. Before we push it back where it belongs, we're going to enjoy the memory and each other and nobody would want us to appreciate this night more than Harmon Turner, the best goddamned quarterback that ever played football in South Dakota—so how about a cheer?"

The guys slammed their feet to the floor and rose in a body.

"All Heart! All Heart! Have we got 'im? Well I guess! All Heart! All Heart! YES! YES! YES!"

I looked at Eric and saw tears in his eyes. I looked toward Titus and his face was wooden. His hands made big fists on the cleared table before him.

Bull took a drink of water, loosened his tie, looked at the water glass and shook his head. Waterboy bounced up and poured about two shots into it from a flask. That brought a cheer. Bull lifted the glass in salute, took a healthy swig and wiped his mouth.

"Okay, we've got some awards to hand out so let's get down to business. The first one goes to the guy who came the longest distance—who claims it?"

Abe Parker stood up.

"It's mine because I live in Los Angeles and two blocks west of Doug Otte, who's the only other guy here with brains enough to live in the greatest city in the world."

Doug waved him down, stood up stiffly and managed to look sorrowful while the gang hooted at Parker's claim for Los Angeles.

"It hurts me almost as much as my broken tail, but I got to put it straight. *I* get the prize because when I drove over to pick up Abe I found I had a low tire and drove back home to leave my car in the garage and he picked us up and that means I drove two blocks further'n he did."

That started a lot of argument ended by Bull who gave the box of crackerjacks to the sore-tailed Otte as a snack to enjoy on the long trip home.

Waterboy won the prize for the guy traveling the shortest distance. It was a white cane so he could find his way home even if he got blind drunk.

There was lots more of that and I drank beer and watched

people. Pat seemed to think most of it was funny and laughed a lot. Florine smiled less and less and a couple times added something to her coffee from a flask she carried in her big black purse. Once she looked my way and lifted her eyes in a "My God" look before sipping some more of her spiked coffee.

Coach Titus finally was asked for a few words and got up slow, walked to the podium like it was a hangman's scaffold and looked over the crowd as they stared back in silence. He looked old. The crowd saw that for the first time and the reactions were mixed. Waterboy looked shocked, Jacobson seemed almost contemptuous, Bull was sad and so was Muggsy. Abe Parker's face was blank, Florine's bored and Ed Folsum just looked expectant.

"You know, it's funny," said Titus slowly. " I didn't want to be a coach. Old Ernie Pearson, our principal, talked me into it. Or bribed me. Offered more money for my teaching if I'd take it on. Red O'Brien had quit after a lousy season and nobody else in school could coach but maybe Miz Hendrickson, who was mean enough but too heavy to demonstrate a three-point stance let alone block and tackle."

That got a few snickers and Titus picked up steam.

"When I called the first practice and looked over the scruffy bunch of half-pints and overweight slobs standing there in crumby uniforms, it about made me sick. You remember the first thing I did?"

"Yeah," yelled Waterboy, "you made us double-time around the field."

"That's right. I figured if eleven of you could make it I might not quit the job. It about broke my heart when you all managed it. I was so dumb then I thought old Bull Dickey was fat and Waterboy might be fast. We didn't have enough guys at that first meeting to hold a real scrimmage. But a funny thing happened along the way. I watched this crappy bunch get their tails whipped all through the first season and I saw them take it and work and bitch and stick it out and when I made my last talk to you at the end of that miserable season I told you you had sure enough lost every game but you had won something more important and that was character. It maybe wasn't much yet, but it was a start and the next year we'd win a couple games. You guys got so carried away you won three. You remember that?"

They did. Loudly.

He talked about their third year and then the fourth and every time he asked them a question the response was louder. When he ended up with the last game and asked if they'd been any good, they rose again with a crash of feet and roared, every man and woman in the room, players, wives, girlfriends and hangers-on. Every face was shining and even Florine was on her feet, not so quick or loud, but with them.

"How about that?" said Titus, and left the podium.

People crowded around him, shaking his hand, patting him on the back and telling him he was a hell of a fellow. He made apologies, saying he had to leave. Bull went down the stairs with him while others gathered in clumps around the cleared tables and talked of football and dances and hot summer nights at the old swimming hole.

Bull returned to the bar, where I was back on duty and stood there, drinking his beer and watching the thinning crowd. When it was down to a few townsfolk, Waterboy and Doug Otte, Bull suggested I join him with the latter two at their table. At first there was some kidding but before long the conversation petered out.

"Where'd Titus come from?" I asked.

"Iowa," said Waterboy. "Sioux City."

"Actually," said Bull, "it was Nebraska and South Sioux City. Just across the river."

"Anybody know anything about his wife?" I asked.

"He never talked about her," said Bull. "I don't know if she died, walked out or what. All I know is he came to Corden with this little girl who grew up fast."

"And you think Turner knocked her up?"

"I said it was possible."

"Hell," said Otte, "it was possible the whole team knocked her up."

"Including you?"

"I was on the team."

"That's all it took?"

Bull shook his head, scowling. "She wasn't that wild. She was crazy about the team and the excitement and needed a lot of affection. She didn't have a mother and God knows Coach never knew how to handle her."

"Man," said Otte, "she was a cat in heat, that's what she was. Tease your joy stick right out of your pants. I danced with her the first time in the Playhouse and about got laid standing up."

"Was that the night Phil Jacobson slugged you?" asked Waterboy.

Otte looked flustered for a moment, took a drink and managed to laugh. "As a matter of fact, it was. He'd had a dance with her right before me and thought he was taking her home. When he saw me snuggling up to her he called me out and while we were trying to beat each other's brains out, Turner took her home or someplace. Probably got into her before we finished our fight."

"How'd Titus feel about his players messing with his girl?" I asked.

"Shit, he never knew what the hell went on with her. He thought she was just as excited about the game as he was, it never came into his head she was just wild about dongs."

"Did Jacobson ever slug Turner over the coach's daughter?" I asked.

"He gave it a try. Turner tied him up in knots, like a Boy Scout with a clothesline rope. You'd swing on him and he wouldn't be there and when you got tired he'd wrestle you. That son of a bitch was quicker'n a trout and had arms like an octopus. I figured he learned that wrestling with girls. Had a lot of practice."

"Tell 'im about the party after the Toqueville game," said Waterboy.

"Ah!" said Otte, shaking his head, "that wasn't all you heard."

"What'd you hear?" I asked Waterboy.

"A bunch of guys got drunk and Bunny was drunk with them and they all went off in the car Phil Jacobson borrowed from his old man."

I looked at Bull. "Were you along?"

He shook his head.

"Who was?"

"Turner," said Waterboy, "and Jacobson, Otte and Parker."

"What happened?" I asked Otte.

He waved his hands. "Nothing. Just a lot of fooling around."

"Yeah," said Waterboy. "Some fooling. And Bunny left town four months later, knocked up."

"Goddamnit," yelled Otte, "you don't know she was knocked up and if she was you don't know it happened that night and you're just sore you weren't in on it."

I asked where she'd gone and they didn't know. Waterboy thought she might've gone to Iowa to see her mother but Bull rejected that, saying she was supposed to have died already. They decided there might've been an aunt or some other relative she went to.

We finished our last beers, said good night to Eric and went outside. The sky had cleared during the party and the Milky Way was a bright speckled path across the black sky. The moon was three quarters full. We walked in silence except for footsteps on the pavement that echoed in the night. Waterboy said good night at First and Main. We went into the hotel. It was quiet enough so you could hear an ant fart.

"There'll be frost by morning," predicted Bull as he headed toward the stairs.

"That's okay with me," said Otte. "I'm sick of cold wet. It quits this drizzle, the whole hunt might turn out okay after all."

I had a feeling it'd take more than clear weather.

ELEVEN

I woke in the morning with a start, thinking I heard the shower and then realized it was only the toilet flushing upstairs. It did it loud enough to echo through the county.

Sunday Bertha slept in and I went to find Margaret. She was poking coals around in the big black range when I entered the kitchen and the fire reflected red on her smooth cheeks and tinted her black hair. She gave me a flashing smile and a good morning.

"It's easier to use the gas range," I told her.

"That doesn't warm the kitchen, but I did use it to make coffee. Want some?"

I did and had hardly settled at the table by the windows when I heard the hall floor creak and in came Joey looking cheerful as a sick bloodhound.

"You forget to go to bed?" I asked.

He ignored me and gave Margaret a begging look. She promptly got a cup, filled it with coffee and put it on the table across from me. He sighed, thanked her and sat.

"I talked with them monkeys in room two last night," he told me. "Managed to wise up the youngster because he's fresh

married and eager as a pup to get back home to his wife. He told
me this farm where they stopped is thirty-five miles from here,
off County C this side of Wickerton. You take a left where there's
a stop sign and drive through a dinky slough and up a little hill
and this farm's there on the right of the road. Name's Jasperson.
Can you go this morning?"

"You want I should skip church?"

"You haven't been in church but for funerals in twenty-five
years."

"But the farmer might."

"All right. Go on time for dinner."

"You paying for gas?"

"It won't take more'n four gallons at the most."

"So you get cheap service."

"All right."

"Nothing's going to come of this," I said.

"Maybe not, but we got to check. Just don't stop to leak in a
cornfield, some hunter might take you for a pheasant."

"Nobody that blind could hit me."

"Blind shooting's what kills hunters most often."

Margaret brought us both eggs, bacon, toast with strawberry
jam and more coffee. Joey, who at first said don't bother, ate
three eggs, four slices of toast and most of the bacon. I
considered letting him know he'd eaten a fifty-cent breakfast but
decided no, it'd make it that much harder to collect my gas
money.

I filled him in on the reunion party, including Waterboy's
claim there'd been a gang bang of the coach's daughter after the
last big game.

"You'd ought to talk with Coach Titus," I said.

He put down his knife and fork and stared a second at his plate.
"I don't hardly see how I could ask him about a thing like that,
Carl."

"Just ask why his daughter left town in the middle of a school
year and where she went."

He picked up his fork and scraped it around the egg yolk congealing on his plate.

"Maybe you could ask."

I shook my head. "You ask. It's your business. I ask, I'm just nosy."

"You asking to be deputized?"

"If you want me working for you, yeah. And paid for it."

"When the hell'd you turn greedy?"

"Well, Joey, I'm getting on. Got to think how I'm going to manage in my dotage."

He said he'd talk with the mayor, thanked Margaret for the breakfast and walked out without remembering to wipe his mouth on the napkin.

None of the hunters went to church. I suspect at least the husbands who had wives along would've made it if Ma had been around but with only my moral influence to weigh on their conscience it was no contest. Florine and Pat put on their finery and went to try and keep at least half their families in God's good graces. Hank got into his navy blue suit, white shirt and striped tie and walked with them, enjoying it to the nines.

When I went out to the kitchen, heading for the garage and Elihu's Dodge, Bertha was sitting at the kitchen table with Margaret. Both looked at me.

"You working for Joey?" Bertha demanded.

"For a couple hours."

"You're supposed to be responsible for this hotel."

"So I'm leaving you in charge."

"You're just going to get yourself in trouble."

"When'd you start worrying about my troubles?"

She didn't bother to answer that and Margaret said it certainly was a lovely morning for a drive.

"Sure. Want to come along? Maybe you could keep me out of trouble."

I expected a rise out of Bertha but all she did was drink from her mug and give me a glowering stare.

"Well," said Margaret glancing at the harridan, "would it be all right?"

"It's Sunday," said Bertha. "Do as you please. But she wouldn't like it."

Margaret smiled. "Will you tell her?"

"No."

She said that, letting us know it was too shocking for poor Ma to survive.

It was around eleven when we set off for Wickerton. The sun stood naked in the clear blue sky and warmed the car in spite of the cold north wind. Margaret's smooth face glowed in the slanting light and I kept sneaking peeks her way, liking what I saw. There were neat, tuck-in wrinkles at the corners of her eyes and laugh lines around her mouth. She looked over the low hills and brown pastures we passed, smiling as if she knew secrets about the land that gave her private satisfactions.

"Where'd you say your daughter was?" I asked.

The smile faded as she turned her head. "I don't believe I said."

"So where is she?"

"West."

"There's a lot of that. Where?"

"California."

"She doesn't keep in touch?"

"We've never been great letter writers."

"What's she like?"

She tipped her head back against the seat and half closed her eyes.

"I think she's very pretty. Her hair's dark, like mine, and she has a lovely figure, not bony like her mother. A very proper girl, maybe a little too serious. Reads a lot, likes good music and makes her own clothes. Always busy. I used to tell her she should have more fun but she said, in her serious way, that she had fun doing what she did. When she was a little girl she made her own paper dolls and all their clothes."

"Sounds like a kid who'd write regular."

"Oh well," she said, lowering her head, "she sends me cards every now and then. I'm the one terrible about writing, that's the problem."

"You mind giving me her address?"

She stared at me. "What for?"

"I'd like to talk with her."

She forced a laugh. "You don't think I ever had a daughter, do you?"

"I'm wondering if you've got one now."

We passed a crossroad cluster of tacky places that offered garage services and groceries, which seemed to capture Margaret's total attention. She even looked back as we moved on.

"Know somebody there?" I asked.

She turned around and answered while looking at the road ahead. "No. Places like that are very depressing, don't you think? There were three houses there. They all must depend on the business that comes to that gas station and grocery, and they can see for miles that no customers are in sight probably twenty-three hours a day. Imagine."

I didn't push her anymore about the daughter and soon we located the Jasperson farm. It was a wind-whipped clapboard house with peeling white paint, the usual front door without a stoop and a side door that would enter the kitchen. The red barn sagged and the outhouses leaned south. I pulled into the yard, which was beat-down earth and a few iron weeds around the edges.

"I'll wait in the car," said Margaret.

The north wind slapped me in the face as I got out and flapped my pants while I squinted around, taking in the distant barbed wire fence on the west side and a scrabby piece of ground someone had tried to make into a vegetable garden near the side door. There was no telling at this stage whether it ever produced anything but I doubted it had been much.

A woman peered at me through the storm door as I approached. The flawed glass distorted her face into a weird mask.

"Mrs. Jasperson?" I asked.

She nodded.

"I'd like to talk with you a few minutes."

"Why?" she asked, looking past me toward the car.

"You had some visitors yesterday morning, right?"

She thought about that, couldn't decide on an answer and shrugged.

"This is serious," I told her. "A man was murdered in Corden yesterday morning. I got to find out all I can about everybody that was staying at the hotel where it happened."

Her hands flew to her face when I said murder and her mouth dropped open. She tried to speak twice before she made it and then she said, "Who?"

"A man named Turner."

Her hands lowered and her mouth closed. She pushed the door open, told me to come in and stood aside as I slipped past.

The kitchen was big, open and neat. There was a cistern pump by the sink and a small wooden ice box in one corner. A white table stood in the center with four straightbacked chairs tucked around it. Mrs. Jasperson's face seen without the distorting glass was very normal, with wide cheeks, bright blue eyes under heavy eyebrows and a wide, no-nonsense mouth.

"Did a man named Bud Kinman have breakfast here yesterday morning?"

"You want some coffee?"

I said yes.

She waved me toward the table and I pulled out a chair and sat while she brought a cup and poured black coffee into it. She filled one for herself and sat down, watching me.

"Why'd you leave the lady outside?" she asked.

"She didn't want to be a bother. Kinman was here, right?"

She nodded and pushed back light brown hair with a touch of gray in it. I guessed she brushed it a lot.

"Where's your husband?"

"Back east. Ohio. His ma's dying."

"You're alone?"

"Uh-huh."

"You've known Kinman awhile?"

She smiled. Her teeth were some yellow but even and the glint of gold showed they'd been worked on.

"All my life. We started first grade together in Wickerton."

"He come around every hunting season?"

"Never been here before in his life."

"So why'd he come this year?"

"I guess you already got that figured out."

"When'd he get here yesterday?"

"About five-thirty. Maybe six."

"Alone?"

"You don't look at all like a policeman."

"I'm a deputy. Temporary. You didn't answer my question."

"I don't like the direction you're going."

"That figures. Just keep in mind my problem's not with adultery; it's murder. I don't care whether you and Kinman talked, held hands or went to bed—I just want to know if he was here, when he was here and it'd help if I knew why. I think I know why."

Her smile was sad. "You think I look like a vamp?"

"You look fine. Want to tell me what happened?"

"He got here at five forty-five."

"You were watching for him, right?"

She examined her cup, took a small drink, put it down and seemed to make up her mind.

"Yes. I was up at four and don't suppose I slept more'n a wink all night, trying to think what he'd be like. He wrote my friend Orah that he'd be coming. I hadn't seen him in over a year or so. Back then we met by accident in Sioux City when I was visiting my sister and we were shopping. He'd just been widowed. We

got talking and wound up having lunch together. My sister went
and had her hair done."

She glanced toward the back window, which overlooked prairie to the edge of our world.

"We fell in love in high school when we were sophomores but
then his folks moved and we lost touch. I been married since I
graduated, or that same fall, and I thought what I had was all I
could expect. My husband's not a bad man, he just doesn't see
me much if you know what I mean. Bud sees me good. You
know?"

I nodded.

She took a deep breath. "Now I got to decide what next. Bud
wants me to go back with him. I want to. But Frank, that's my
husband, his ma's dying and he thinks the world of her and I
can't see just going off and him coming home to an empty house
after his other loss, but I can't see staying here after what I've
found is possible and it's got me up in knots because I'm not a
loose woman or all selfish or at least I never thought I was
anyways but I can't think long about anything but Bud and me."

I remembered Kinman's looks and it was hard to imagine their
romance. Without looking up she asked if I thought she was an
awful person.

I said no.

Her head went lower. "I do," she whispered. "I think I'm just
awful."

"You're mostly unlucky. Where'd Kinman's friends go while
he was with you?"

"Into town. That's where my friend Orah lives with her pa and
two sisters. They gave them breakfast. Orah's been my best
friend since school too. She knows Bud."

She was silent for a moment, then sighed. "Orah thinks I'm
crazy. At least that's what she says but really she envies me."

"Okay," I said, "before you make up your mind which way
you're going to jump, you better remember if your boyfriend
doesn't come clean on where he was yesterday morning, he could

be a murder suspect. Especially if it turns out he knew Turner. You know if he did?"

She looked up, frowning. "Was that the football player from Corden?"

I nodded.

"I don't see how Bud would've known him, no."

"He got around a lot. You never met him either?"

She shook her head. "Just heard the name some years back." She thought some more and looked at me with wide eyes. "You think Bud might be arrested?"

"He might."

She stared around the kitchen as though she'd never seen it before. Finally her eyes met mine again.

"And I could give him an alibi?"

"If you don't, he could be in deep trouble."

"And Frank'd know I'd been with him."

I could feel her weighing it all. If Frank would inevitably find out what had happened, then there was no use in her staying home to comfort his return and her testimony would save Bud and he'd be indebted to her and she'd live happily ever after. She looked at her hands which were clasped together on the table, and shuddered.

"Oh, dear Jesus," she said softly, "I don't know. I just don't know—"

"You think Bud Kinman maybe knew Turner, don't you?"

Her head jerked. "No. No, I don't think that at all. Leave me alone now. I have to think. I can't talk to you anymore. Go away. *Please.*"

I thanked her for her time and the coffee, and left.

TWELVE

Margaret's head jerked up as I came out of the house and I saw her make swift movement of something in her lap as I walked toward the car.

"That was quick," she said as I slid in behind the wheel. "Any luck?"

"What were you doing while I was in there?"

"Just making notes for a shopping list tomorrow."

"You planning big surprises on the menu?"

"Wait and see. What happened in there?"

I started the car and said, "She says she gave the man breakfast and maybe a little more yesterday."

She listened without comment as we headed back home. When I'd covered it all she remained silent while staring out the window at the prairie. Finally she turned toward me.

"Did you find her attractive?"

"A little stocky for me."

"She seems to have been very confiding. Did you comfort her?"

"I listened."

"You didn't wipe her tears or pat her a little?"

"Nope."

She turned in the seat and leaned her back against the door.

"You don't like Kinman, do you?"

I admitted that.

"It galls a man to see a woman who's attractive and involved with a man he thinks isn't good enough for her, isn't that right?"

I supposed so.

"Were you sorry you brought me along?"

"Lady," I said, "if I'd felt like making a pass it wouldn't have slowed me a tick knowing you were out in the car."

I caught the gleam of her teeth as she smiled. "No, I bet you wouldn't. You're all instant action and impulse, aren't you?"

"Like any other man."

"No." She shook her head. "No, you're not at all like any other man. You're unique."

"Nobody's that."

"Maybe not, but you come closer than any I've met."

"I guess you haven't known many."

"I've known enough. If I've got trouble, that's not it."

I couldn't figure whether she was coming on to me or just making fun and still hadn't doped anything out when we pulled up in front of the hotel.

Joey was in the lobby with Hank when we walked in. There was no one else around but the canary and he wasn't saying anything either. Margaret and I went into the hall and hung up our coats. For a second we stood there, looking at each other, then she nodded and walked back toward the kitchen.

I entered the lobby and sat on Elihu's chair.

"Well?" said Joey.

"Kinman got to the Jasperson place about five forty-five according to the lady of the house. She was alone and he had breakfast with her and maybe spent some time upstairs. Farmer Jasperson was off with his dying ma in Ohio. The lady doesn't think Kinman knew Turner, or says she doesn't. I'm not sure.

She knew who Turner was from when he played against her high
school. Now she's trying to figure out if she's willing to be a
witness for Kinman or stay with her husband. She doesn't figure
she can do both. I'd guess she'll stick with her husband. She's
Lutheran."

"How come you took Margaret along?" asked Joey as if he
hadn't heard a word I'd said.

"She wanted a ride and I figured the company'd keep me
awake. I also figured she'd make it easier to talk with a farmer's
wife but she didn't want to go in so I'll never know."

Joey considered me for a while, glanced uneasily at Hank and
finally stood up.

"Well, thanks anyway. I'll talk with the fellas again when they
get back from the hunt."

"He thinks you're trying to hustle Margaret on his time," said
Hank as the door closed behind Joey.

"He would."

"You got any idea what you're doing?" asked Hank with that
wiseguy look he knows annoys me.

"Not usually."

"You're doing just what Grandma figured when she told you
you'd get nowhere with Margaret."

I swiveled the chair and scowled at him. "Why? You think
she's got ideas about a good woman reforming me?"

"You hit it."

"The trouble with you," I told him, "is you got this notion
everybody's trying to puppet everybody else around, just like
you."

He ignored that. "The trouble is, Grandma doesn't understand
Margaret."

"And you do?"

"I think so."

"Tell me about it."

"She likes to make people interested in her. She tamed old

Bertha in about five seconds. Told her she had wonderful green eyes. You ever notice Bertha had green eyes?"

"That's a reflection from her gums."

"Come on, they're not that bad. And she really does have green eyes but nobody notices she's anything but fat. Margaret told her she was the most efficient person she'd ever seen. That she never made a false step or a wasteful move."

"You shove around the lard Bertha does, you can't afford extra steps."

"What'd Margaret say that made you feel special?" he asked.

"Nothing," I lied.

"No? But she got you to take her along on the trip this morning and you came in here from the car with your eyes glazed. She maybe didn't tell you you were special, but she let you know some way that's what she thinks. She's going to jump you through the hoops."

I turned to look out on the street. "For such a smooth operator," I said, "you got a special way of making folks love you. It touches me deep somewhere. I think I'm sitting on the spot."

"It'll be interesting," he said, "to see how she reacts when you make your pass."

I sighed, thinking of the days not far back when this kid thought maybe I was almost a hero. That was when he was five years old. Or maybe six. By the time he was fourteen his grandmother's perspectives had taken over. I've heard it's common for respect to skip generations and wondered if maybe Elihu put so much space between himself and his folks just to keep me from gaining any alliances. It always made me wonder that I never heard him or Ma talk about their parents. It was like they came into being, all whole, in Corden, South Dakota, and never were kids or knew about growing up. They never spoke about anything before they were married and I was born.

Or hadn't I listened?

Hank give up ragging me and went to the kitchen to talk with

Bertha. He could sit at the table out there while Bertha was slapping together supper, never make a move to help, and talk steady or pump her dizzy without ever making her snappish. She even listened to him and answered his questions. I could only guess she looked on him as the kid she never had.

I was watching Gabriel pick seed from his food tray in the green cage when I saw movement out front and went to look. Three cars pulled in from the south and parked in a row before me.

The first thing wrong I noticed was Phil Jacobson's car was being driven by Bull Dickey. Next to him was Ed Folsum. Bull got out moving slow and stiff, glanced my way and shook his head. Parker got out of his green Chevy and came around in front of Phil's car with Muggsy right behind. The big surprise was seeing Gustafson and Downer, the Iowa men, getting out of Parker's car and joining the crowd around Bull.

I went to the door, shoved it open and asked what had happened.

"Phil's dead," yelled Waterboy. "Murdered!"

THIRTEEN

"**H**ow'd Gustafson and Downer happen to be with you?"
Joey asked Bull Dickey. The three of us were sitting in the dining
room booth. Phil's body was over at Doc Feeney's office.

"Gustafson couldn't get his car started and his friend, old sad
eyes, asked if maybe we had room for them and I said sure, they
could ride with Ed and me. Gustafson was so grateful I wished
I'd said no. So the four of us were in my Buick, Phil had Otte,
Swede and Waterboy in his Olds and Abe, Coach Titus and
Muggsy were in Abe's Chev. We took off in a caravan heading
south to the Simpson farm off County J where Phil knew the
territory best."

"That's east of the slough and swimming hole?" I asked.

"Actually Simpson owns land east and west of that whole area.
We started on the west side, where he has his biggest corn field.
Right away Gustafson volunteered himself and old sad eyes
Downer as post men to stand at the far end and scare up birds we
drove their way. Phil squelched that right away. He said he and
Coach'd handle that job since he wasn't about to have a couple
galoots he didn't know getting the best crack at the birds when for
all he knew they couldn't hit a barn door."

They had spread out about thirty feet apart and started along the rows. The fields had been frozen on top but stayed wet under and the footing was murder. Before long mud gathered in big globs on their boots and they were stumbling and slogging like a pack of drunks in a swamp. The few birds they saw ran like lizards, close to the ground.

"All survivors," said Bull. "The ones that've learned if you run you live, if you fly you die."

At noon they went back to the cars for bag lunches Bertha and Margaret had prepared and for coffee Bull brought in a gallon thermos.

"Gustafson pulled out a whiskey flask," said Bull, "and I told him if he poured an ounce he'd not carry a gun the rest of the day. He said considering the luck so far he'd be as well off, but he stowed the flask and behaved."

"He talk any about himself?" I asked.

"Yeah. Mostly about what a great hunter he was. That galled Muggsy, who said we'd all heard what a great scrapper he was too, letting him know we'd all heard of his run-in with you. He said you hit him when he wasn't looking and Muggsy asked which time. All he did was grin and shake his head. Then Waterboy said he heard Gus was a great lady's man and that wiped away the grin. Gustafson got a mean look and told us Margaret hadn't been so standoffish in Iowa. He said she might act like the high virgin here but she'd had a baby without a husband back home and God hadn't had a hand or anything else in it. Phil got sore about that, being a good Catholic, and let him know he wouldn't hold still for more of that blasphemy. Things were getting so hot I broke it up and split the gang. I took Gustafson, Waterboy, Downer and Swede with me while the other guys went their way over on the field near the slough to the east and we went west."

Hunting improved for Bull and his crew after that but stayed lousy for Phil and the others. For reasons not clear to Bull, Phil got the notion they might find prairie chicken around the slough and they moved into the edges there for a while but came up with sniffles. Finally Otte got disgusted, unloaded his shotgun and produced a flask. Muggsy and Abe joined him. Phil and Coach Titus wandered around the swimming hole area, where they got separated in the trees and brush. About then Bull and his group returned to the rendezvous point in the parking area above the swimming hole and went to relieve themselves out of sight of the road. By four they were gathering beside their cars. Gustafson passed his flask around and everybody was having smokes and bitching about the hunt when Otte looked around and asked what the hell happened to Phil Jacobson?

"Went to shit and the hogs et him," said Waterboy, who always said that when anybody was missing.

Otte didn't think that was funny, got up and hollered for his buddy but there was no answer. After some talk about where he'd been seen last, several of the guys wandered toward the swimming hole and Waterboy remembered there'd been a sign down in the marshy area at the north that warned of quicksand. Nobody knew who'd put it up and there'd never been any stories about people being caught in it. Bull, Otte, Coach Titus, Muggsy and Swede went to check. They found Phil stretched out, face down, a couple yards south of the sign. When they turned him over there was a red hole where his right eye had been. He was cold dead.

Somebody said they had to get him out of there and they hauled him up to Phil's car and put him in the back seat and came tearing back to the hotel.

Joey didn't bother to tell Bull he shouldn't have moved the body and of course the hunters had tracked up the whole area so we couldn't have found a sign if the killer'd been an elephant.

Mayor Syvertson called Aquatown and tried to talk Baker, their chief of police, into coming to help investigate the crime. Baker was no more interested in wandering around sloughs than in catching pneumonia. He told Syvertson why import help when he had Wilcox right on the scene?

"He says you're the best murder man in South Dakota,"

Syvertson told me, standing there beside Joey, whose hound dog expression would make a first sergeant choke up.

"You're being conned," I told the mayor.

"No sir, he was sincere. You're the man and you're here and you owe this community and I'm deputizing you and you'll get what you were paid when you subbed for Joey."

"I still got a hotel to worry about."

"You never worried about it when you took off before and as long as Bertha's around and has help from Hank and the new woman, they can manage."

So I said, what the hell, fine. If Joey was grateful for my sacrifice he hid it well.

FOURTEEN

"**N**ear as I can tell," said Doc Feeney, "he was struck from behind with a rock. I suppose he fell on his face and the killer rolled him over and finished him off."

"With a slingshot," I said.

He shrugged.

I looked at Joey. "You ever talk with Titus about his daughter and the team?"

"No," he said, meeting my look straight on. "I didn't want to any more'n you do."

I sighed and suggested we talk with the gang bangers we still had alive. That gave us Abe Parker and Doug Otte.

Florine opened the door when I knocked on room nine. Her face was painted like she'd spent the day at it but the trimmings didn't hide her fear. Looking over her shoulder I saw Abe sitting hunched on the bed.

"We'd like to talk with you downstairs," I told him.

He stood slowly, looked around the room as if trying to find something he'd lost, and walked past his wife. They didn't speak or look at each other and I heard the door close firmly behind us as we started down the stairs.

Abe slid into the dining room booth, folded his hands on the table and met Joey's gaze.

"What we want to know," said Joey, "is what happened ten years ago, the night after your last football game with Corden High. I want it straight."

Abe leaned against the booth back and for half a second closed his eyes.

"It's kind of foggy," he said. "If you haven't been through it, you don't know how it gets after a day like we had. We were all like drunk through the last half of the game, hell, maybe from the opening kickoff. All I know is, I never had such a high in my life. We just scrambled those poor bastards. They dropped the first kick on their own two and Bull nailed the quarterback on their first play and got us a safety. The first time he got the ball, Turner ran sixty yards for a touchdown. We went crazy. When it was over, Coach Titus took us all to dinner and we were laughing and yelling and ribbing each other like a bunch of maniacs—"

He rubbed his cheek and jaw, licked his lips and took a deep breath.

"After supper a few of the guys, like Swede, who always had to get back home and slop the hogs or milk the cows—they went. The rest of us wandered over to the pool hall and people were slapping us on the back and whooping it up. Some of them offered us drinks and we swigged it straight or put it in Coke. Then we went over to the dance and it was more of the same except of course there were girls and they were all friendly and Bunny Titus insisted on kissing every player on the team and everybody thought that was great and some other girls did it too. Bunny was the only one that went around in back of the dance hall for drinks with us and she was mostly with Turner, who was feeling her up in the dance hall and kissing her when they went outside and she was feeling wonderful and kept telling us how great we were. Then Phil went and got his old man's car and a bottle he found in their pantry and we all piled into the car—"

"Who's 'we'?" asked Joey.

"Turner, Otte, Bunny and me. There was another girl, Dona May Albright, who was gonna go but got scared at the last minute and backed off. She was with Muggsy and they both decided we were all too drunk."

"Where'd you go?" I asked.

"The swimming hole. We parked off the road there over-looking the water and took turns drinking from the bottle and kissing Bunny. Pretty soon Turner got her pants off and then she decided to take off everything and said we could all have her but we'd have to draw straws to set up the order and Turner went off and cut lengths of iron weed and held them for us to pull and we made our picks and he got the long one. That made us mad because we figured he cheated but she said it was okay, he was her number one guy."

Parker mopped his face and wasn't meeting Joey's eye anymore. His face was red and sweaty.

"Turner took his time and the rest of us got too excited and hadda hurry too much and wanted to do it more but Bunny got tired and mad and cried. She said Otte was a bastard because he got too rough and everything went sour. We took her home and all agreed we'd never tell what happened no matter what but I think Otte blabbed to somebody."

Joey's face was almost as red as Abe's and his big fists were clinched white on the table.

"You know if she got pregnant?" I asked.

"Well, God, I'd think so, with four guys getting a shot, one was bound to hit."

Joey made a strangled sound and I quick asked, "You think Bunny told her dad?"

"No. She never told him anything and he was too busy with football to ever ask."

"You know any guys not in the gang bang that were specially nuts about Bunny?" I asked.

"About half the school, I'd think. Waterboy was goofy about her, partly because she was small enough so he didn't feel like a shrimp around her and besides she always called him cute. Swede was moony about her and Bull had a case too. He tried to pretend he was just worried about her being too wild for her own good but I think it was more than that."

"You know if Turner'd laid her before?"

"Oh yeah, sure. Lots of times. And maybe Phil too. She sure's hell wasn't cherry that night."

"How'd she feel about Bull?"

"I think she kind of liked him but he made her tired, always trying to make like her old man, you know? She told him she already had one father and that was one too many. When he tried to keep guys from giving her drinks behind the dance hall, she told him to mind his own business."

"Did Bull say anything to you guys?"

"No. It kind of surprises me when I think back. I guess being the biggest and strongest of us all, he didn't think it was fair to throw his weight around. Bull's a weird guy. Thinks too much."

"Ever talk to Coach Titus after the game night?" I asked.

He hadn't. Not on any personal level and certainly not about Bunny. She left town after Christmas vacation and none of the gang ever saw her again.

"Could you tell she was pregnant when she left?"

"Nah. But we heard. Dona May blabbed to a friend that Bunny missed a period or two so it figured. In the spring Titus resigned and left town in June."

Joey managed to push thoughts of the gang bang aside and told Abe to go through everything he could remember of the hunt. He said it started okay with lots of kidding about the mud and no birds but that got old quick. Gustafson and Downer were no help since Downer was gloomy enough to sour Christmas and Gustafson couldn't keep his mouth shut. He had ideas about how everything should be done and Phil had come down on him three times, letting him know he was a goddamned alien and wasn't going to be in charge.

Abe wasn't about to account for where people were while Phil was gone. When Joey asked if nobody moved off together to take a leak, he got indignant and asked what'd Joey think? They were a bunch of women?

Finally Joey gave up. "Tomorrow we'll go out and run through what happened right on the spot with all you guys. You think about what you did and what others did and you noticed. Was anybody in a real bad mood, did you see anything special about how guys acted when they found the body. Stuff like that. Okay?"

"Nobody in our gang did it," said Abe. "It had to be somebody else. Where was that guy Kinman and his crowd?"

"What makes you think Kinman'd have anything against Phil Jacobson?" I asked. "They know each other?"

"Hell, *I* don't know. But you guys should, what the hell you been doing if you didn't check 'em out?"

"Don't start giving me any guff," said Joey. "A man who's just got through telling us what you told's got no damned business getting righteous with people trying to straighten up the mess you've made. Now go send Otte in here."

Abe glowered but did as he was told and Otte soon took his place in the booth. At first he flat denied there'd been any gang bang. Joey let him know we'd heard different from Abe and I'd already heard enough from others so we knew he was lying.

"Now come off the bullshit and tell us what you remember."

Otte jerked around enough to hurt his sore tailbone and after sweating some said okay, he'd been along but it hadn't been his idea, he hadn't got Bunny drunk and he'd only put the blocks to her because everybody else did and he didn't want to hurt her feelings or look gutless to the other guys.

"That was damned sweet of you," I said. "We heard you were so rough on her you spoiled the whole damned party."

He denied that with volume and heat. Joey let him rave a little and suggested maybe he'd just as soon not have everybody in the hotel hear him mouthing off and he shut up quick. After some more horsing around he confirmed what Abe had told us. But he insisted he had *not* been rough, just maybe a little hasty.

He didn't remember ever seeing Bunny after that night and yes, he heard she went away to have a baby and it sure seemed likely it was planted that night but it could've been earlier because Turner'd had her regular all fall.

He was willing by then to talk a week but Joey was so mad he cut him off and sent him back to the lobby.

FIFTEEN

Joey kept steaming while I rolled a cigarette and smoked about half of it. Then he took a deep breath, leaned against the booth back and asked if I would kindly go and question Titus. He was too down to face the man or hear anything more about what he'd been digging into. I finished my smoke, butted it out and left him cradling an empty coffee cup and nursing his disillusionment.

The overcast sky make it dark, cold and windy out. Titus was staying at the Bergstroms' place, just a block north of the hotel beyond the Congregational church. Bergstrom had a spare upstairs bedroom with an outside stairway more like a fire escape than a proper approach. I went to the front door and Bergstrom's woman answered my knock and told me the coach was up in his room and I could take the inside stairs up. There were other bedrooms but nobody used them since all the kids had grown up and moved.

I tapped on the last door on the right and it opened almost at once, as though he'd been waiting for me. His lean, hard face was clean shaven and his bristly hair looked brushed but untamed. His bright eyes took me in with an expression I couldn't figure. He was like a different man than the one I'd talked with at the party.

"I need to talk with you," I said.

"Oh? Man to man, or cop to suspect?"

I managed to keep my jaw from dropping and worked up a grin. "I seem like a cop to you?"

"No," he said, taking a step back to admit me, "but then, I can't believe Phil Jacobson and Heart Turner are dead either. What do you want to talk about?"

I parked on the straightbacked chair by the bureau as he went over and sat on the bed's edge.

"Why'd your daughter leave Corden High and go to Iowa?"

"What's that got to do with murder here and now?"

"That's what I got to find out. Joey and I've been talking with Abe and Otte. They told us about a party after your last big game."

"Yeah," he nodded casually, "I took 'em all to dinner. We had a big time. Noisy, but reasonable."

"I'm talking about a different kind of party after that. After they'd been to the pool hall and then the dance and wound up at the swimming hole. Four of them, with your daughter."

He gave me his hard, football coach stare. "What're you trying to say?"

"I'm saying we heard she was drunk and so were the guys and things got wild. Now two of the guys at that party are dead. If we don't find out what happened all down the line, two more might get it. You want to help us out?"

"What do you mean, things got wild?"

"They say there was a gang bang."

"You believe it?"

"It doesn't matter a damn what I believe. I want to know if you know what happened, if your daughter was pregnant when she went to Iowa and, if so, who do you think might've been torn up enough to start killing people."

"You think I killed my boys?"

"Did you?"

He'd been leaning so far forward he about came off the bed but suddenly he settled back, folded his arms and lifted his chin.

"No I didn't. If I believed all that shit, I might have. And I think it's a goddamned shame that grown men'd tell tall stories about a girl who's been dead for ten years and can't speak for herself and that you'd come here and tell me such a story. I notice Joey didn't come. He wouldn't do a thing like that."

"Coach, let's not dance around with all this bullshit. I'm not a man that thinks a girl's the devil's own because she had too much to drink and liked boys too well. What I want you to level with me on is, was the girl pregnant and, if not, why'd you hustle her to Iowa? That's all. You going to tell me?"

He glared at me a few moments, then recrossed his arms and straightened his back.

"She went to see her mother, that's all she told me. She wasn't pregnant I know of. That's not the kind of thing she'd tell me about."

"What did she tell you about?"

He started to speak, swallowed and blinked. Finally he shook his head. "She told me when she needed money and when my tie was crooked."

"And when she got pregnant."

He brought his square hands down and gripped the edge of the bed. "Yeah." That came out in a whisper as he looked away from me. "I gave her hell for staying out all night and she told me what'd happened. She'd lay everything out when I made her mad. She did it with all the guys so I couldn't make Turner marry her. I knew she was going to have a baby before that. I'd told her she was gonna marry him by God or I'd run him out of town with a bullwhip. The awful thing is, she wanted to marry him but she wouldn't do it when he was trapped like that. I lost my temper and told her she was a slut and slapped her and the next day she went to Iowa and her ma, who was living there in Colstrom."

"Her ma was Margaret, right?"

"Yeah. She tell you?"

"She told me her daughter lived in California. She didn't say anything about you."

"Yeah, well, she wouldn't. I never did anything right with a woman in my life and that's a fact. Don't understand them. They just screw up my mind till I'm hog-tied. Margaret was too young for me—or I was too old for her."

"What did happen to Bunny?"

He swallowed a couple more times and rubbed his face. "She died. Baby was stillborn and Bunny cut her wrists in the bathtub a week later and let her life flow down the drain. I guess it was my fault but I don't know what I could've done. When she went to Margaret I thought maybe together they'd work things out okay but she wasn't much good either. I heard she went with lots of guys. Margaret, I mean. You can blame me for what happened to Turner and Jacobson but I didn't kill 'em myself. I couldn't ever done that. Well, maybe nine years ago, yeah. But not now and not sneaky. Anyway, I couldn't blame them for it all. Not once I thought about it. They were just dumb, horny kids. It's all just a goddamned sad mess."

"Out of the guys she knew that weren't at the swimming hole that night, who'd you think was craziest about Bunny?" I asked.

He got up and walked to the window. "I thought about that a lot since yesterday morning. It seems like just about all the team was crazy about her. Waterboy, Ed Folsum, Swede and guys that weren't even on the first team. None of them are crazy enough to be killing off the party gang. I can't believe that for a minute."

"Wasn't Bull Dickey one of her fans?"

He thought about that so hard he almost came out of his misery. "He warned me more than once she was wild," he admitted. "He didn't say it that way, of course, he just hinted around that I'd ought to pay her more attention, keep track of her, you know? I asked him, flat out, what the hell he was getting at and he just said she was an awfully attractive and loving girl and guys might take advantage of her. I asked him if he figured she and Turner were going too far and he tried to back off that but I got the picture and tried talking with Bunny about being careful with guys and not getting involved with just one at her age."

I could pretty much imagine how subtle he'd been and how well that had gone over with Bunny.

"You resigned as coach because of all that, didn't you?" I asked. "It wasn't because all your first team was graduating."

"That's right. I'd had it with the school and Corden in fact. Guys wouldn't look me in the eye. They either figured I hated them or they pitied me. I couldn't stomach that shit."

I'd had about enough myself and was about to thank him and leave when he suddenly gave me his hard look again and said he heard I'd gone for a trip that morning with Margaret. I admitted she rode with me out to where I questioned a woman.

"How'd you make out?"

"The farm lady told me what I wanted to know."

"I meant with Margaret. You get into her?"

"No."

"Must be slowing down. From all I've heard, I figured you'd made out quick."

"I don't think she's the kind of woman you're saying she is."

"You don't, eh?" His bitterness came back in a blink. "Maybe you're not as smart as they say. Take my advice. Use a rubber. You might catch more'n a cold."

"You hate her because she was too young to be the wife you wanted?"

He went over and sat on the edge of the bed again.

"I'm sick of it all, and that's it. You want to arrest me for murder? Go ahead. I don't give a shit. Either do it or get the hell out."

I got the hell out.

SIXTEEN

Hank was sitting at what Elihu called the salesmen's desk when I came out to the lobby after supper. It was a solid oak rectangular table with a two-foot-high divider across the center covered with signs behind glass advertising town stores and products. Elihu played solitaire on his side and now and then salesmen actually used the other side to write up orders or work out their swindle sheets. Hank was writing a letter, most likely, I guessed, to a girl up north.

People came and went and a few stopped to talk but most kept moving. When it was down to Hank and me, Margaret came in. She'd let her hair down from the bun and it made her about ten years younger. The glasses were gone and she was wearing lipstick. Not the plastered stuff, just enough for color. Hank lost interest in his letter as she strolled over to the window facing east and said it looked as if it might be clearing up.

"Let's take a walk," I said.

She looked at Hank and smiled. "Willing to watch the lobby?"

Her smile would have made him wax the floors if she asked and his head bobbed as he grinned back.

She got her coat, we went out, did a left and headed toward the west hill. The air was still and dry.

"Where are we going?" she asked.

"It'll depend on you."

She glanced my way. "You mean how far we go?"

"That's right."

She laughed and moved enough so her shoulder brushed mine light as a butterfly wing.

"I'm not," she said, "a long-distance walker."

"I've been talking with Titus," I said.

"Oh?" She drew away and the voice was even more distant.

"He says you were his wife."

She looked ahead and lifted her chin a notch. "I assumed you knew."

"I don't think so. At any rate, I'd only guessed before."

She looked at me with arched eyebrows. "How'd you happen to do that?"

"Everything seemed to fit. Why'd you pretend your daughter was still alive?"

"I like to think she is. You think I'm crazy?"

"No."

"You think it'd be more normal if I were bitter, like Titus?"

"He got a first name?"

"Of course. It's Irwin. He hates it. He prefers the title Coach. He even wanted me to use it. I never did. I just called him Titus or You."

"I guess you weren't together long."

"Long enough. You think I killed those two men? Is that what this walk's about?"

"Joey thinks you're tall enough."

"To reach over the partition from the bureau? I suppose so, I never tried it. I'm not particularly agile. Can you imagine me climbing that thing?"

"It's easy. You just heist yourself up enough to sit, then swing your legs around."

She walked along, looking at me and back at the sidewalk. At that moment we were in mid-block and there wasn't enough light for me to judge her expression.

"You're not serious, are you?" she asked. "I mean, do you think I was a tomboy and grew up climbing trees and shooting a slingshot? I was an only child, a girl who grew up under parents old enough to be my grandparents. I was four when they first let me climb stairs by myself. And how in the world do you think I got out to the swimming hole and killed Phil Jacobson?"

"Maybe you and Titus worked things out together. You do the guys in the hotel, he handles the ones outside."

"That's ridiculous."

We were approaching the corner light and I could see her better. Her face was angry.

"I don't understand you," she said with heat. "I thought you were a little more than half smart. What you're suggesting is just stupid."

"Yeah," I admitted, "it doesn't sing for me."

"Is this one of your practical jokes? Just trying to get me upset?"

"No. I'm trying to figure every angle. With a murder as wild as this, common stuff doesn't get anywhere. Nothing much does."

"Well, don't take it out on me just because you're frustrated."

"Come on, Margaret, the business of you being here now just naturally jerks the long arm of coincidence out of its socket, you know? How'd you hear about the job?"

"Mrs. Dickerson told me. She belongs to the Old Timers Club your parents belong to in Aquatown. They play bridge together and Mrs. Dickerson was originally from my town and knew I was at loose ends and suggested your mother write to me and she did and we met and I came. That's all there was to it."

"How come you mentioned a slingshot?"

"What else could it be? Everybody in Corden knows there was

a steel ball in the head of the men killed. Nobody threw it, spit it or has a gun that shoots balls these days. What's left?"

I admitted it didn't leave much and we stopped a moment at the corner where the streetlight showed her face and the dark hair soft around it.

"You look damned good," I told her.

It took a moment for the smile to come. "You don't exactly have a poetic tongue," she said, "but thanks."

"Did you wear your hair in a bun to fool Ma?"

"It was to make her believe I was sincere. Which I am."

"About what?"

"Everything."

"You're taller than most women I've known."

"Does that bother you?"

"It throws me some."

"Are we going to walk on?"

I said okay and we did but there wasn't much conversation for a while. Finally I asked her how come she married a man so much older than she was.

"He asked me. And at the moment I thought I wanted to get away from my parents. I'd been tied to them too long; people were beginning to call me an old maid and I hated that."

"You weren't all that gone on Titus?"

"I respected him. He was a sincere teacher and seemed awfully involved in everything he did. And his attitude toward me in the beginning was very flattering. I felt special."

"What went wrong?"

"It was never right. I couldn't feel like a real person with him. I realized after a while that he was actually afraid of me and eventually that made him hate me. He couldn't understand why I cried and never asked."

"Why'd you cry?"

"Because I married an old man."

"You had a baby."

She gave me a look of contempt. "I didn't say he was impotent."

When we were away from streetlights I asked if she went with other men.

"Not while we were married, no." She looked at me with her chin high. "I was a proper wife as long as it lasted and when I had to go home and care for my ailing parents I was through with him."

"Even the kid?"

"I couldn't handle her and my parents too. At least that's what Titus said and the judge, who was his friend, agreed and they took her away from me. I tried to hire a lawyer but there wasn't one in the county who'd help me and I had no money so I lost her. A woman has no real rights, you know."

I knew. Women, mavericks and misfits buckled under or ran away. I thought of putting my arm around her but sensed she wasn't ready. When we reached the end of the houses we walked a ways beside the road until we crested the hill. The wind out of the north came on strong and chilling. She folded her arms across her breast and shuddered. I decided what the hell, and put my arm around her.

For a moment she didn't acknowledge it, then she leaned into me lightly and turned her face my way. I tipped my head, put my hand on her cheek and kissed the wide mouth. It was soft and warm. Her hand touched my cheek. Then she withdrew, looking at me. I kissed her again.

"You're very calculating, aren't you?" she said. "One would never guess it to look at you."

I had both arms around her and tried calculating but couldn't think of anything but hurry.

"What now?" she whispered.

"We better go back."

"I can't take you to my room. Bertha would hear."

"The parlor," I said.

She put both hands on the back of my head and gave me a kiss that made my head hum and my ambition rise. I knew she could feel it. When I came up for air she laughed and so did I.

We walked back to the hotel pretty sedately considering the urgency and entered the side door that opened right next to the parlor. I kissed her again inside the dark room, led her to the couch and told her I'd be right back.

The lobby was deserted. Gabriel was asleep under his cover and only the counter light glowed dimly by the register. I walked back to the foot of the stairs and listened a moment, then moved into the darkness. She pulled me down beside her and for a few moments we worked up the excitement and got out of clothes. I found that long and slim is as arousing as round and ripe and sure never found a woman more active or eager. She made soft sounds and I felt so damned appreciated I about killed myself trying to give and take everything possible and something beyond.

When it was all worked out she got on top and gently fondled my face and some more and hummed. I couldn't get the tune but it was better than purring and when I felt her shaking I got my hands on her face and found no tears. She was laughing.

"What's so damned funny?"

"Imagine your mother," she whispered.

I said I couldn't.

She pushed her face between my chin and neck.

"I never knew anybody could do it that many times. I thought once was all."

"Nobody ever did it that many times before."

She burrowed in a little more. "Do you always do it lots of times?"

"Never a dozen."

She laughed softly. "It wasn't that many."

"Whatever. I was too busy to count."

We bragged some more and I knew I liked her about the best of any woman I'd known and wondered if it happened that way because she was older or was it only because I was growing up?

After a while she rose and I stayed still while she tucked the blanket around me. Then she kissed me good night and was gone.

I remembered what Coach Titus had said about Margaret and other men and considering how much she enjoyed loving, it was hard to believe she hadn't known a lot of it. Part of my problem was, I couldn't believe a woman who came on to me that strong was very fussy. But in the end I couldn't believe she was as active as he tried to make me think. It seemed more likely he'd been too old for her and hated her because of that alone.

SEVENTEEN

I headed for the kitchen early, wondering how Margaret would be the morning after. There was no question in my mind how Bertha would be if she'd caught a whiff of what happened and I sweated some knowing how alert she could be.

All was serene around the ranges. Bertha greeted me almost civilly, Margaret looked but kept a discreet expression. I had trouble not grinning like an idiot while trying to let Margaret know I was grateful.

"What's the matter," demanded Bertha, "you look like you swallowed a prune."

"Everything's dandy," I assured her. "It's seven-thirty A.M. and nobody's found a corpse yet."

"You haven't talked to anybody yet."

"So feed me while I'm still innocent."

She snorted and went about her business with eggs and toast while Margaret brought me a quartered orange. As I thanked her Hank came through the swinging door and said I was wanted on the telephone.

I took an orange quarter and walked down the hall, chewing on it.

The caller told me she was Miz Hendrickson. I remembered she lived in the two-room apartment next to the parlor and felt a chill, thinking maybe she'd been kept awake by sounds on the parlor couch the night before.

"I couldn't sleep," she said, increasing my anxiety, "I've been thinking about the boys killed."

"Yeah?"

"They were both students of mine, you know. Phil Jacobson and Harmon Turner."

I wiped my orange sticky fingers on my pants and said sure.

"They weren't model students. Phil was about average, maybe a little above. Harmon was distinguished primarily by a desperate need to be popular and of course his athletic talents."

I waited while she thought a moment.

"O. D. Dickey was my only outstanding student. Had a fine mind. I'm very proud of the way he turned out. He teaches, you know."

"Does he give you credit?"

"I imagine he does. Certainly he should. I nurtured his intellectual interests. Not many do in a town like Corden."

"God knows," I agreed.

Her tone turned waspish. "Don't condescend, and don't pretend a piety you don't feel."

"God forbid."

It wasn't hard to picture her shaking her gray head.

"You're never going to change, are you?" she said. "A rascal from birth and compulsively insolent. Well, I suppose I either woke you or took you from the breakfast table so I'll get to the point. We all know Joey Paxton's qualities are limited to a certain cautious integrity and dogged persistence, and while these serve him well enough under usual circumstances, a great deal more than that is needed at this juncture so you're obviously the last resort. Come over and talk with me. I want to know what's going on and tell you a few things you probably ought to know."

I said I'd be around as soon as I finished breakfast. She wasn't satisfied but said very well.

Bertha was satisfied. She told me my eggs were overdone, my toast was hard as slate and she was right on both counts. The coffee scalded me.

I went out in the thin morning light and walked the half a dozen steps to Miz Hendrickson's door. She took her time answering and I felt the chill of the north wind through my sweater as I stood waiting.

She finally opened the inner door, peered at me a second, as though suspecting I might be an imposter, and finally unlatched the storm door.

I slipped past her into the warm combination living and bedroom and took a seat at the card table she used for dining. The place smelled of coffee and rolls, bath powder and faint cologne. She'd had her silver hair waved and brushed to frame her round face full of wrinkles. Without asking if I wanted any she poured coffee and offered cream and sugar. I took it all, stirred it up and drank. It was scalding hot and stronger than Bull Dickey. She saw me wince and said, "Always try a spoonful first. That way you don't get burned. You've never had the good judgment to test the way first, have you?"

"Afraid not."

"You stay remarkably young for a man who's lived such a dissolute life. I suppose it comes from a dedication to never growing up."

"You haven't changed much yourself," I said.

She waved impatiently. "What can you tell me about these murders?"

I told her what I could, rolled a cigarette and added cream to to the coffee until it was drinkable.

"You think the killings come from what was done to Coach Titus's girl?"

"Maybe."

"Are you going to wait until the other two are killed before you do anything?"

When I gaped at her she smiled thinly, put her forearms on the table and clutched her left wrist with her right hand. Her fingers were ringless.

"Did you know Bunny Titus?"

"I saw her around, I guess, but didn't notice. That was before she turned ripe."

"Yes," she said with sarcasm, "you wouldn't have noticed her before the blooming. You were probably gone during her last two years. She was a pretty thing. And knew it. Flaunted herself shamelessly. I rather disliked her at the beginning of her first year in my class. She seemed hopelessly shallow and foolish. But she surprised me several times, first by how well she read aloud. I make my students do that, you know, it tells me a good deal about them. She didn't stumble or mumble or go too fast. It was as though she respected the writing. I doubt that she did, but she had a pride and she was not stupid and I think she had contempt for the students who read badly and wanted to show them how it should be done."

"The boys went for her, didn't they?"

"At first I think she rather frightened them. All but the most aggressive boys. Harmon was never frightened, he didn't have the imagination for fear. He was probably like you that way, only he didn't have a father he had to escape."

Her brown eyes watched me for a reaction and I rewarded her with lifted eyebrows.

"She ran around with Harmon a lot," she resumed, "but she flirted with the others, mostly boys on the football team. I think it was to annoy her father as much as anything. Coach Titus was a great believer in the strange notion that athletics demanded celibacy, like the priesthood. The only thing Bunny and Harmon had in common was a need to make everybody love them. And of course they were both uncommonly attractive."

"Where'd you hear about the party at the swimming hole?"

"I'm not going to tell you."

"So why'd you want to talk to me?"

"I can tell you what I know without going on about my sources. This isn't a court of law, we're discussing a murder and you're a man with a record of solving a few cases to one degree or another, although I'd hardly pretend I think you can rival Sherlock Holmes."

"I haven't had as many cases yet."

She managed a smile but it had no warmth. "I doubt that you'll survive long enough to achieve his talent."

"Okay. So who do you think is knocking off these guys?"

"Who has a motive comparable to Coach Titus?"

"I don't know. Who was stuck on Bunny besides Turner and Jacobson?"

"James Wilson."

"You mean Waterboy?"

"I mean James Wilson. That's his name. And Abe Parker—"

"Isn't that Abraham?"

"He was christened Abe. Now will you let me get on?"

"Shoot."

"O. D. Dickey and Ellis Eckerson. Bull and Swede, to you."

"What was the matter with Muggsy Bertrand and Doug Otte?"

"They were afraid of her. She was too bright for boys like that."

She warmed my coffee from the pot and for a moment we were silent, thinking.

"Bunny have any girlfriends?" I asked.

"One. Marlis Nelson. A typical best friend of the school belle, plain, overweight, good-natured and funny."

"She the one works at the creamery?"

She nodded. "Does their bookkeeping and other jobs for her father."

I probed more among the list of suspects but she added nothing that helped.

"The truth," she confessed, "is I don't want it to be any of them. I'm not sentimental, but I take some pride in my ability to judge character and none of them, as I knew them back then, seem capable of cold-blooded murder. I never cared anything for Coach Titus but again, I can't believe he ever cared that much for his daughter. Of course having his whole world collapse after his glorious year might have twisted his mind since then."

I thanked her and stood.

She looked up at me. "I've never understood one thing about you. The running away always made sense to me, but why in the world did you always return to Corden?"

"I've got a lot of answers to that one, Ann Rose, but the only honest one is, I don't know. Okay?"

She blushed when I called her by her first name. She probably hadn't heard it spoken since the last time she'd seen her mother, maybe half a century back. For a moment I thought she was going to reprimand me again for impertinence but finally she let slip a genuine smile, stood and said she hoped I'd be able to stop the murders.

"I don't think I care if you solve them, I guess I'd rather you didn't."

I thanked her again and left.

EIGHTEEN

After lunch I hiked up the west hill to Nelson's house and Marlis answered my knock. At sight of me her blue eyes opened wide behind the heavy glasses and then she smiled, showing dimples and laugh wrinkles.

"Well," she said, "Carl Wilcox. I thought you'd never call."

I must have looked pretty dumb because she laughed till her cheeks jiggled. "You've chased every other girl in Corden, I figured I was overdue."

"I was waiting for you to grow up."

"I never grew up, just out. You want to come in?"

"If you've got a minute."

"I could spare a month. Come on."

I followed her through the vestibule and into a maroon-carpeted living room full of bulgy furniture, big wall pictures and her fat father. He peered at me over half glasses from an overstuffed chair in the far corner. His eyes were slits in his broad face and they glittered in the lamplight.

We exchanged greetings and he stirred a little to suggest he knew he should get up but realized I was a reasonable man and would know what a strain that'd be so wouldn't mind if he didn't.

I paid him back by not going over to shake hands.

"So," he said, "you're back in Corden now."

"Been a while," I said.

"Yah. Taking care of the hotel for Elihu, I hear."

"More or less."

"And helping out Joey Paxton on top of it."

"You keep in touch."

"Oh yah. So, you come to see me or Marlis?"

"Marlis."

"Yah, well, I didn't figure I was a suspect in your murders. You want to talk to her alone? You can go in the kitchen."

Marlis giggled and led me through the dining room and into a large open kitchen with a solid oak table at dead center. I accepted the inevitable coffee, rolled a smoke and looked at Marlis sitting across from me. She leaned her elbows on the table, framed her round face with her chubby hands and looked coquettish.

"I hear you were pals with Bunny," I said.

"Oh yah," she said, mimicking her father's accent.

"Were you with her the night after the big football game, ten years ago?"

"Sure. At the beginning. We went to the game together and around some after that. I didn't go to the dance."

"Was she drunk?"

"No. A little tiddly, maybe." She was still smiling but it had lost something.

"How come you didn't go to the dance?"

The smile left entirely. "Nobody ever asked me to dance."

"You didn't go along to keep her company?"

"She had the whole damned football team for company, she didn't need me."

Her eyes avoided me and concentrated on her coffee cup and hands. The hands were smooth and nicely shaped. The nails had been neatly polished.

"She tell you what happened that night?"

She glanced up and back at her hands. Finally she nodded. "Tell me."

"I swore to her I'd never tell anybody."

"Somebody's killing guys. You want them all to get it?"

She hunched up her shoulders and bowed her head further. "It'd serve 'em right. Especially that Doug Otte bastard. He hurt her."

"She say he did it on purpose?"

"She thought so, yah."

"How about Abe Parker?"

"No, he was okay. Up till Doug she thought it was all pretty great. Bunny was an awful bad girl. She wanted all the guys and all at once, or thought she did till they tried it and then she found out it was a mess. None of 'em really cared about *her*, you know, they just all wanted what they wanted and it was like she was a common bottle they were all passing around."

She thought a little, hugged herself and peeked at me, suddenly smiling. "It was more like she was a bottle they were all filling, huh?"

"How drunk was she?"

"Drunk didn't have anything to do with it. I mean, it wasn't like she passed out and they all helped themselves. She led 'em on, you can bet."

"Her father says she took them all on so he couldn't pin her pregnancy on any one guy."

"That's just what she told him. It was sort of to make it all right for her doing it with four of them, but really I think she just wanted it that way. She'd rather Doug hadn't been there, she said she wished it could've been Waterboy because she knew it'd make him awful happy and she thought he was cute. I think it would've made him crazy. I never saw a boy more nuts about somebody than he was about Bunny. Only, you know, he was nearly as crazy about Heart Turner. It was kind of weird, like he had a crush on both of them."

"Had Bunny slept with all those guys before?"

"Bunny never slept with anybody. I think she made love with Heart. There might've been another before him. She kind of hinted around to me a couple times but never came right out and told me."

"Why not? Sounds like she told you everything else."

"I figure it was with a guy she wasn't so proud of, you know? Somebody she fooled around with when she was real young, like maybe thirteen. She fooled some with little boys when she was only five. I don't mean any that young really did it, but they showed each other's parts and kissed a lot. Bunny was kissing crazy."

"She kiss you?"

She blushed and after a moment, nodded.

"What she wanted most was to be married and make love every morning and every night and maybe once at noon. She thought Heart'd be the one but worried some because he didn't seem too smart and he liked other girls and she didn't think he'd amount to much. She wanted a guy that looked like him that everybody thought was wonderful and smart as Bull Dickey."

"She mess with Bull any?"

"Oh no. Too ugly. But she liked to kid around with him. Bunny was really crazy, I guess you know that by now."

"So Titus sent her to Iowa. Was she going to keep the kid or have an abortion?"

"Well, at first she was going to have it and keep it but when she started getting big she got scared and told me she was going to get rid of it—"

"You saw her after she left?"

"No, we wrote letters. Almost every day. I burned them all as soon as I read 'em. So anyway, she was going to get rid of it only then it moved and she told me she was in love with it."

"You think Turner was the father?"

"Yah, most likely. She'd missed a period before she took on the gang so that's not when it happened. Actually, that last year I didn't see her much more than at the football games when Heart was playing. She didn't have much time for me like when we were sophomores and juniors and spent hours talking to each other in our bedrooms. But after that night with the guys she came over and we talked just for hours. Something happened to her that night. It was like she'd always been crazy about ice cream sodas but finally had too many and they made her sick. That sounds dumb, I guess, but that's the way it was. The more she thought about it the more she thought guys that'd watch each other do it were real bums and she didn't like any of 'em anymore."

"But it was her idea."

"Yah, but she didn't like herself anymore either."

She sat back and folded her arms under her big breasts. Her round face became gloomy and aged years.

"She said I was lucky I didn't have guys chasing after me. I was better off, she said. She wasn't really dumb but she said a lot of really dumb things. Why you think she did that?"

I had no answer and she didn't expect one.

"When'd you hear from her last?"

"Oh," she said, "a couple weeks before she died. She wrote a letter from her mother's and told me I'd always been her best friend and confidante. That's the word she used. I was like her father confessor, is what I was. She never understood me one bit, she couldn't. She was never fat and homely a minute in her whole life. Oh, she got fat pregnant, but that's not the same. She was still beautiful, I bet."

"I guess you still miss her?"

She leaned forward on the table heavily and nodded. "Oh yah," she whispered. "Oh yah."

She was clouding up to cry and I quick asked if she'd ever met Bunny's mother. She brushed her eyes with the back of her hand and shook her head.

"Did Bunny ever write about her?"

"Some. She said she was beautiful and nice."

"She say anything about men her mother went with?"

She shook her head. "Bunny wasn't a girl that'd tell you about anybody else except how they acted toward her. I mean, if her mother'd been messing around with guys and didn't get meals or wasn't around, she'd have mentioned it. But if the guys didn't mess up things for Bunny, she wouldn't notice them."

"Do you know that Bunny's mother, Margaret, is working at the Wilcox Hotel now?"

"Yah, I heard about that. Even saw her over at the grocery once. She's real slim and tall. Kind of severe looking I thought, but maybe it's because of her hair being up tight."

"Did Bunny give you any idea of how her mother felt about her?"

"Sure. She said she was crazy about her. Everybody was always crazy about Bunny except her pa. That old bastard was the only one didn't love her. That made her real unhappy. I tried to tell her if he didn't love her he wouldn't give a damn what she did and she said all he wanted was to boss everybody. That's why he was the football coach. He was God and they all loved him for it. So he loved them more than he did her. I guess she sort of wanted to show him they wanted her more than him, if you know what I mean."

I felt about then I'd never know what any woman meant but nodded wisely and said maybe we'd talk again sometime, and left.

NINETEEN

Joey spent a good share of Sunday trying to find Heart Turner's kin and finally came up with an uncle in California but the man said he couldn't come to Corden for the funeral. When Bull heard of the problems he volunteered to make arrangements for a memorial ceremony on Monday and the burial in our Catholic cemetery north of town.

I'd guess it was the biggest funeral Father Patterson ever ran and while he looked tight in the beginning he began to relax along the way. By the time he got to the eulogy he was sailing.

He told us that Harmon Turner, known to all his fans as Heart, had been a victim all his life. Everybody thought he was a hero and happy but every day he suffered because of his weakness and his weakness was not physical but spiritual and moral.

"Here was a boy, glorified and spoiled because he could carry, kick and throw a football better than any of his peers. He was admired because he could run around, over and through other boys like himself. We put him on a pedestal. Our newspaper devoted columns to his exploits. Girls flocked around him, boys wanted to imitate and emulate him."

He paused and glared accusingly at his audience.

"What was it all for? What did it bring him beyond the excitement of the moments when he was triumphant on the football field and in the back of automobiles?"

Some mouths dropped at that. Even mine sagged a little.

"I'll tell you what it came down to," said Father Patterson, "it came down to a boy who never became a man. A boy who was only successful as a womanizer. A boy who died with a ball of steel in his brain on the floor of a shower room in a grubby hotel. Murdered, no doubt, for his weakness. Harmon's body was heroic, his athletic prowess was exceptional, but does anyone here know what sort of mind was in that handsome head? Or what kind of a soul lived in that fine body? *I* don't know. Nor can I. Ever. You're wondering, how can I talk of him like this with his body here before me? I can and do because he was a lovable boy and an admirable athlete. But life calls for more than that for any soul to be complete. None of us is strong enough to go through life on the weak support of muscle and agility. You must have power that comes from belief, faith and fidelity."

He went on from there, pushing us to use the inner eye which, he said, never weeps. I thought it over later, the difference between our Protestant ministers and this priest. All the Protestants I knew would've milked the sympathy and tragedy for all it'd yield before moving to penitence and higher goals. Old Patterson socked them without indulgence, trying to shock his flock into thought.

The only trouble was, a high percentage of the gab I heard leaving the church sounded more indignant than thoughtful. The citizens generally had more faith in muscle than soul power.

I caught up with Patterson before he got into his house and he greeted me with something shy of enthusiasm, saying if I wanted to know what sort of confessions he'd heard from the late Mr. Turner, I'd find it as fruitless as when I'd come around about the Foote family.

"For one thing," he told me with obvious resentment, "he

never came to confession. He never came to me on his own in his life."

"You just baptized him, huh?"

"That I did."

"But a few young ladies maybe came to confession about him."

"I'll not talk of that and you know it."

"Okay. But I got a notion during your talk that you figured Turner was a bad influence so maybe you'd be willing to allow that and give me some idea of what people in town'd have reason to want him dead in a grubby hotel's shower room."

He smiled ruefully. "I didn't mean to be offensive, but certainly you don't think of the Wilcox Hotel as grand."

"All it's got," I granted, "is clean and Bertha. I'm not here to bitch about that."

"I didn't think you were. But in answer to your question, I *did* see Harmon as a pernicious influence. Not because he was truly evil, he wasn't, but because of what he came to symbolize in Corden, his existence became a force of evil among us."

"You own a slingshot, Father?"

That didn't crack him up even when I explained it. When I asked if he knew Marlis Nelson he shook his head, saying she wasn't Catholic. Neither was Bunny Titus.

"So you wouldn't know a thing about them?"

"Carl, I know little enough about my own flock. Certainly in a town this size I know a great deal about people of other, or no, faiths, particularly ones as conspicuous as Bunny Titus. She was a bright star in a relatively dull sky."

He wasn't quite satisfied with that line and thought about it a second. I waited and he looked at me questioningly, as though he hoped I'd say it was fine.

"Marlis thinks Bunny had a lover even before Turner. You ever get wind of anything like that?"

"No, thank the Lord. Any before Turner and she'd have been a child."

"I heard she liked boys from when she was five."

"Well, liking them within reason is no sin."

"From what I hear, Bunny wasn't much for being within reason. Who else from the team crowd came to your church?"

"Abe Parker and the Folsum boy, Ed. I think all the rest were Lutherans, more or less."

I headed back toward the hotel and went to visit Miz Hendrickson again. It took a while for her to answer the door and I figured I caught her in the bathroom because she looked so flustered when she finally showed up.

She reluctantly invited me in but didn't offer coffee.

"Who sat near Bunny in your class?" I asked.

"Well, let's see. I always arranged things so boys sat next to girls. Started that when I taught primary grades and it worked fine because most boys are afraid of girls and it cut down on whisperings and such. Of course it didn't work all the time with the high school group but you'd be surprised how often it did. Anyway, O. D. Dickey was on her left and the Eckerson boy was behind. Alfie Elrod, another farm boy, was on her right and she was in the front row where I could keep an eye on her. She was a handful, I'll tell you."

"Did Bull talk to her?"

"O. D. was a very well-behaved boy. I never had any cause to fuss at him. Bunny whispered to all three of them. Alfie mostly just grinned and blushed. He was afraid to talk to her even when class wasn't in session."

"How about Swede?"

"He was shy too, but I think now and then he'd respond. He could do that more easily than the others, of course, sitting behind her like that."

"You know if Bull and Swede were both in Bible school with Bunny?"

"Oh yes, I'm sure of that. I knew that fine young missionary, Homer Altman, who taught the class at least two summers, it must've been twelve, thirteen years ago—maybe more. My goodness, back when they were in junior high."

She went on a little more about that but didn't tell me anything useful so I thanked her and drifted.

I walked toward Boswell's shack hoping that Doug Otte and Abe Parker were being careful to stay in a crowd. The weather had cleared, leaving the sky bright and the air dry and breezy. Fields that had been mud Sunday were blowing dust and the cornstalks were rustling and crackling in the crisp air.

I let myself into Boswell's place, which was a little more cluttered than ever but saw he still kept the small table, sink and bunk clear. He was stretched on the bunk, dozing easy with his mouth open yet so silent only his rising and falling chest let me know he was still alive. As I cleared papers off his chair and sat down, he opened his eyes, made a nodding motion and slowly sat up.

"You were still a janitor up at the school fourteen, fifteen years ago," I said, "right?"

He groped around on the table by the bed for his pipe and tobacco, loaded up, lit it, sighed and reached for his glasses, ready to face the world.

"Sure thing," he said.

"Remember Bunny Titus?"

"Sure." The pipe went out, he tamped it down with his stumpy forefinger and relit it.

I asked which guys had been most gone on her and he said just about all. "She was all flouncy and bouncy."

"How about when she was just in junior high, before she got involved with Turner and the other guys? Was she special before she sprouted?"

He thought about that some and began to nod. "Yeah, back when she was mostly skinny she went for the farm boys. Alfie Elrod and Swede Eckerson. They was real shy. She liked that then. Got a kick out of gettin' 'em all flustered. She was feisty from the start. Saw her muss Alfie's hair once and he blushed so hard I thought he'd bust a blood vessel. She wrestled Swede down once out on the school grounds during recess. He let her do it. Got him down and sat on him and tried to make him say enough. She had to hold him down a long time before he did and I knew he coulda got up anytime he wanted."

"You think they ever had a chance to mess around alone?"

"Nah, they were just kids funnin'. Kids like that, it's like they were playing with pets. There's nothing more to it."

I remembered there'd been a hell of a lot more to it, even before I knew what it was.

"When did Swede get close to the girl he married?" I asked.

"Don't remember he ever did. I mean at school. The gal he married went to school somewhere else. Toqueville, maybe. I think he met her the summer after the big game. Don't remember ever hearing of the wedding. Suppose it was with a J.P."

"Marlis Nelson, Bunny's old pal, told me she thought Bunny'd gone all the way with somebody before Turner. You think it could've been with Swede?"

"I don't hardly see when he'd had the chance, even if she'd wanted to. He's not the kind that'd start things himself, like Heart, and he never had no time. Either school or working, that's all he had."

"He found time for football."

"Yeah, he had that. But even there, he missed lots of practice. Coach wouldn't've put up with it with anybody else, but Swede was so good and dependable, Coach just went along. He sure knew Swede wasn't off lollygaggin' around."

"Marlis guessed Bunny might've done it with somebody she was ashamed of later. Could that be Bull Dickey?"

"I suppose it could've been with about any boy given the right chance. But I don't see Bull. He was always too sober, and I don't think anybody in Corden'd be ashamed of getting close to him."

I thought about it all some, turned down coffee, moonshine

and beer and went to get Elihu's Dodge for a trip to the Eckerson farm.

Eckerson's place was on a low rise and had a bedraggled windbreak of box elders and elms along the north side. I wheeled up the dirt road to the front, parked and got out. A scruffy brown and white mongrel dashed toward me from the barn, yapping, circled me half a dozen times and when I stood still and stared at him he sat down, let his tongue hang out and grinned like a happy moron.

I looked up toward the house and saw a woman behind the storm door. As I started toward her the dog came to his feet and trotted along.

She opened the door and stepped out, pulling a gray shawl around her hunched shoulders. Light brown hair straggled around her cheeks and down her slender neck.

"What is it?" she asked. "Has something happened to Ellis?"

"Not that I know of. Can I talk to you a few minutes?"

"I can't buy anything."

"I'm not selling anything."

"Well, what do you want, who are you?"

"Carl Wilcox, I'm—"

"You from the hotel in town?"

"That's right—"

"Stay right there," she said and slipped back inside and out of sight. I looked at the dog, who gave me a slobbery grin.

The next moment Mrs. Eckerson was back at the door, carrying a carbine.

"Now, you just go back to your car and get out. You think I don't know how to use this, just try me."

"I guess Swede's been talking about me—"

"I know all about you. Git."

"Okay, tell him I called."

She had her finger on the trigger and started raising the gun. I turned and headed for the car. The dog didn't follow. As I started the Dodge I looked back at the stoop and the woman was still there, holding the carbine ready. I waved and drove out.

I kept telling myself that being run off a farm shouldn't cause a man to feel embarrassed even if it's done by a woman but I couldn't quite figure out how I could describe the experience to anyone without feeling some shrunk.

TWENTY

The hunters returned to the hotel a little before suppertime. No outsiders had been with the team gang and Doug Otte and Abe Parker had been in the center of old classmates all day long. I met them on the sidewalk and heard the shooting had gone well. Only Otte and Parker had failed to get a bird and no one kidded them about it although I did overhear Waterboy crack that they'd been saving their ammunition for self-defense.

I stopped Swede as he moved away from Bull's car, heading for his own Model T, which he'd driven in from the farm.

"In a hurry?" I asked him.

"Well—"

"I went out to your place this afternoon," I said. "Your wife ran me off with a carbine."

He nodded thoughtfully.

"I figure you told her not to talk with me."

"That's right."

"What were you afraid she'd say?"

He looked past me at the men going into the hotel, then lifted his lean jaw. "Nothing. I just let her know how you been with women."

"Did she know Bunny Titus?"

"Never laid eyes on her."

"I hear you might've laid quite a bit more on her."

His face flushed. He scowled. "Who told you a thing like that?"

"Actually, nobody. I did hear you knew her pretty well when you were in Bible school together, and that she sat in front of you in school."

"So?"

"I wondered if you heard about the party after the last game, when Bunny and a few guys went out to the swimming hole."

He flushed again. "That was none of my business."

"But you heard about it?"

"I suppose. It was a long time ago."

"Seems like somebody thinks it's fresh. Two of the guys involved are dead. The other two are stepping careful and all you guys are keeping them protected. I guess you know what happened back then, and what's happening now."

"What's that got to do with you getting run off my farm?"

"That's what I'm trying to find out. I'd like to come out to your place with you now and talk with you and your wife. I can come with Joey tonight, if you'd rather. How do you want to do it?"

Most of the men were in the lobby by then except for Waterboy, who stood by the door, watching us.

Swede looked at him and called, "Whyn't you go over to the beer parlor. I'll be along."

Waterboy nodded, stuck his head inside the lobby to speak with someone and then walked by us, nodding at me.

"You might just come by the farm after supper," said Swede to me. "Sometime before nine."

"But after dark?"

"That don't matter. Let's leave Joey out of it."

I agreed. He went over to his car, cranked it up and took off, heading for the farm. I watched the car go out of sight, walked to the beer parlor and took the stool next to Waterboy.

"Where's Swede?" he asked.

"Went home. Got stuff on his mind. You know how close he got to Bunny back before Turner was her big moment?"

The barman delivered a beer to Waterboy, asked what I'd have and moved off to draw another.

"He got about as close as two feet, when he was sitting behind her in old lady Hendrickson's English class," said Waterboy.

"I hear he was pretty gone on her."

"We all were, so what?"

"I can't help figuring somebody was really crazy about her. Enough so he's still crazy and killing people. I'm not saying it's Swede, I'm just trying to cover the odds. How'd *you* feel when you heard about the gang bang at the swimming hole?"

"Left out," he said, grinning.

"That's all?"

"What more?" he demanded, sobering. "You figure they forced her? Like hell. And don't shit me, Wilcox, you'd have been the first in line given the chance. She was *something*. Give you a hard-on with a pout and if she smiled you'd blow. You couldn't blame anybody for taking a shot given the chance."

"How about Turner and Jacobson getting killed? Nobody to blame for that either?"

"Come on, killing's a hell of a ways from screwing. Although, when you come down to it, Turner was bound to get it sooner or later. The only thing is, he should've got it in the act, when he was coming. He'd have died grateful. Dick in and balls up you might say."

"What about Jacobson?"

"Well, he didn't make a habit of asking for it. With him it's harder to figure. I don't think it had anything to do with the night of the big game."

"How do you feel about Otte and Parker?"

"Otte I could do without and I like Parker's wife better than her husband. What I'd really like is a Parker House roll, if you follow me, and if you do, I'd rather you came behind than before. Catch?"

"I doubt a snake could follow you in his own burrow."

"I'd hope not."

Parker and Muggsy showed up with their wives and Waterboy went to join them, pulling over a chair to the edge of their booth. I drank most of my beer and drifted back to the hotel.

"Well, Sherlock," Bertha greeted me as I came into the kitchen, "you got it all solved yet?"

"Yup. Know everything but who did it and how to prove it."

Margaret gave me a secret smile and I started getting ideas but after dinner she got busy with Bertha making sandwiches for the next day's lunches and I didn't get any chance to make suggestions for later.

I drifted over to City Hall and found Joey sitting at his desk looking pained so I knew he was thinking. I told him of my trip to Eckerson's in the afternoon and Swede's invitation to an evening's chat.

He dug up a grin. "You better hope Swede's home. You catch his wife alone and she'll likely put a hole in you."

"I'm not too sure I'd be any safer with him."

"Anybody's safe with Swede. That's the most reliable man near Corden. I bet he wouldn't shoot a gopher."

"Then how come he's got a carbine in the house?"

"In case a wolf comes to the door. One like Wilcox."

It was getting on toward dusk as I headed for Eckerson's farm. I could see a light in the kitchen from a good ways off and when I came up the drive saw the dog loping out to meet me. He barked on a harmless note and nuzzled my legs as I got out and walked toward the kitchen door. Swede showed up dark with the light behind him and shoved the door open as I approached.

I went past him into the house and smelled good stew, fresh bread and rich coffee. His wife wasn't in sight. He waved me toward the table and I took a chair while he sat across from me. He'd been drinking coffee and his cup was almost empty.

I asked how the hunt had gone. He said fine.

Steps came down the stairs and his wife appeared in the doorway. I was glad to see she wasn't carrying the carbine.

"My wife, Dora," said Swede. "This is Mr. Wilcox."

I said pleased to meet you and she nodded and asked did I want coffee and poured it when I said yes. She pushed cream and sugar my way, filled Swede's cup, then stepped back and leaned her haunches against the counter. She'd brushed her hair since I'd seen her last. I decided she wasn't a bad-looking woman. A little plain but not homely, with small features, blue Scandinavian eyes and pale skin. Her mouth was a little tight.

There was no point in making polite conversation about how the farming had gone this year or if he liked our weather. The farming and weather had both been horseshit and grasshoppers weren't worth talking about. So I tried another tack.

"You ever see your husband play football?" I asked Dora.

She shook her head.

"Where'd you two meet?"

"County Fair," she said.

"When?"

"September. After he finished high school that June."

"Tell me about it."

She looked at Swede. He looked at me. She pushed away from the counter, went to the stove, filled a cup with coffee and came over to sit down on my left.

"You going to want our whole history or just the high spots?"

"The high spots." It didn't seem likely there'd be many.

She said she worked at a Lutheran church booth cooking hamburgers during the fair and Swede ate a lot of them and they had wound up going to the grandstand show the last night and before Christmas they were married.

"So you never knew any of the football gang or what made your husband a hero?"

She looked at him again. "He didn't even tell me he knew Heart Turner."

"You'd heard of him, huh?"

"Everybody'd heard of him."

"How about Bunny Titus? Everybody know about her?"

"She was talked about some." She examined her coffee as though expecting to find a bug in it.

"I don't guess Swede was one of the talkers."

She glanced at me swiftly, then down again. For a second I thought I saw something near a smile. "No," she said, "Ellis hasn't ever been much of a talker."

I turned toward him, hooked my arm over my chair back and asked if he remembered the missionary teacher, Altman, from his Bible school days.

The question seemed to surprise him and for a moment he stared at me, trying to figure my angle. Finally he said yes, he remembered the man.

"You were in his class with Bunny, Bull and some of the other guys that later played football. Did Bunny's reputation as kind of a free roller begin then?"

"What's a free roller?"

His expression was blank but the tone let me know he was offended. I groped some. "In high school she had a reputation for being pretty wild," I said. "Easy to get."

He considered that, pushed his coffee cup left, then right and hunched his shoulders. "She liked boys early," he admitted.

"How'd she like you?"

His wife watched him with narrowed eyes but he didn't look her way.

"Okay," he said.

"Why'd your wife run me off this afternoon?"

He looked at her. "Why did you?"

She flushed. "I've heard enough about him not to trust him when I was alone."

He looked back at me. "I guess you'd ought to understand that."

I wasn't sure whether I should be proud or sore but managed to smile. "I'm not all that dangerous. Talk to women every day without getting either one of us in trouble."

Neither of them looked impressed.

"Okay. You both know about the murders. Joey and I figure one of the team guys did them because he was in love with Bunny and wanted to get them because they caused her death, one way or another. We're trying to figure out which of the guys was that crazy about her. For now let's say neither Joey or I figure you'd kill anybody but the guys are dead and somebody you know must've done it. Who was that crazy about her?"

"You're asking Ellis to point his finger at one of his friends?" asked his wife.

"If he's got any notion who it might be, damn right. If we don't find out, two more of his friends could get murdered."

"So maybe they deserve it."

She said that with such heat Swede's head turned her way and for a second he stared at her. She kept her eyes on me.

"You're saying you wouldn't blame a man for killing in this case?" I asked.

"I wouldn't. They acted like animals. Got off scot-free, lived while she was dead and I'd bet they never lost a minute's sleep over it."

"You think it was rape?"

"Of *course* it was rape! You think any girl'd do that willingly? Never!"

I looked at Swede. "You agree?"

He took a deep breath, crossed his arms and tipped his head back. "I don't believe Bunny was bad. She was reckless, is all. Shouldn't been drinking. That was the trouble."

"And the guys took advantage of her."

"That's right," said Mrs. Eckerson, bobbing her head.

I stuck around a little longer but didn't get anywhere and when I got up to leave Swede stayed with me to the car.

"Don't mind Dora," he said. "She gets worked up."

"She only worries me when she's got a gun."

I stopped by the car and faced him.

"Just between us guys, did you make out with Bunny when you were kids?"

"I wouldn't known how."

I figured she could have shown him but decided it wouldn't be smart to say so.

"You think," I asked, "that Coach Titus might be the killer?"

"Well now, I hadn't thought of that." The way he said it I didn't believe him, and I felt maybe he didn't want me to.

"Now you have, what?"

"Well, I suppose he'd have the best reason, wouldn't he? I don't suppose he ever thought she was bad."

"He told me he called her a slut. And let me know her mother was no better than she'd ought to be."

"He could still hate the guys for it."

"Yeah, but he's pretty old to be climbing on bureaus and working a slingshot."

"I don't know. He looks in good shape."

"Where do you keep your old slingshot?"

"Slingshot?" he said, looking innocent.

"Don't tell me you never had one. On a farm, I'd think you'd keep it around for gophers and the like."

"I use a twenty-two."

"And your wife uses a carbine, huh?"

"Only on traveling salesmen."

I looked for a grin but he didn't own one so I said good night and left. He was still standing in the yard, watching as I looked back in the mirror and headed for the county road.

TWENTY-ONE

"Things have been going on since you left," Hank told me as I entered the lobby. "Kinman's crowd came back from hunting without him. And Otte's checking out in the morning. Going back with Jacobson's body to California."

I sat down and started building a smoke.

"Parker still around?"

"Uh-huh. But Joey's been trying to convince him he'd ought to go too. Warned him he couldn't protect him."

"What'd Parker say?"

"He paid for a hunting license and he's staying till it's expired. What'd you find out at Eckerson's?"

"That the female of the species is more deadly than the male."

"Really? You think Swede's wife is the slingshotter?"

"Probably not. But she'd sure be cheerleader for anybody doing it."

"I can't believe Swede's the one."

I wasn't about to try convincing him and went over to City Hall looking for Joey. He wasn't around so I headed toward Eric's Café and finally found him at the beer parlor.

He was standing by Parker at a table with Florine, Muggsy and Pat Bertrand. Parker was looking sullen, his wife had a glow I figured came from a bottle, Pat was bright-eyed and Muggsy just looked worried.

When I approached the table Parker looked up at me and jerked his head at Joey. "Your town cop's trying to run me out of town."

Joey stood looking down, wearing his usual hangdog, sad expression. "I'm asking you to be reasonable, think of your own good and yeah, mine too. It'd be a big help if I didn't have to worry about you. I can't park in your pocket or sleep by your door—"

"Damn right. What happens'll happen. If your killer's made up his mind, he'll get me here or back home and I'd rather settle it here."

"Where's Otte?" I asked Joey.

"Playing pool with Bull Dickey and Ed Folsum. He's leaving in the morning."

"How about Titus?"

"Haven't seen him."

"Is he hunting with you guys tomorrow?" I asked Parker.

He nodded.

"You mind if I come along?"

"Why not? Just don't get in my way."

Joey, who knows how I feel about hunting, gaped at me. Florine grinned. "So," she said, "the manhunter's gonna be a watchdog, right?"

"I can goddamn take care of myself," said Parker.

"I'll see you in the morning," I said.

Joey walked out with me and we stopped under the streetlight on the corner, where I told him of my visit with the Eckersons. I asked if he knew Dora, Swede's wife.

"No. She's a woman keeps to herself. Only comes to town for groceries and clothes. Needs a kid. All's she got is Swede and that dog of theirs. He comes to town with her and sits outside the stores, grinning at everybody."

"Swede?"

"No, the dog."

We walked past Eric's place and I glanced in to see Waterboy at a table with Titus and Ed Folsum.

"Well," I said, stopping.

Joey turned and halted. "Huh?"

I tilted my head toward the café and Joey looked in. His long face stretched still more. When I suggested we go in he nodded.

The three men looked up as we approached. Waterboy grinned, Folsum frowned and Titus was deadpanned as a poker shark.

"You on the wagon now?" I asked Waterboy.

"I ride 'em all—beer, booze or garbage. You know how that is, right?"

"Yeah," I admitted. I thought of telling them I'd be on the hunt with them in the morning, then decided no, if they were hatching plans it would be better to surprise them. I asked what they'd been talking about and Waterboy said fishing. That didn't seem too likely since I was pretty sure neither of his partners had ever held a rod or a pole but neither of them corrected him and it was obvious they'd run out of gab for now.

Back on the street I asked Joey if any of the guys he'd questioned ever offered a hint about who they thought might be nutty enough to kill Turner and Jacobson over the gang bang of ten years ago.

"Only Ed Folsum. He finally said the most likely'd be Coach Titus. The only trouble, he admitted, was he couldn't believe Titus had ever been interested in anything but football so it didn't seem likely he'd go nuts about what happened to his kid ten years ago."

"I don't remember anybody mentioning Folsum's having anything to do with Bunny. Did you ask about that?"

"Sure. Nothing doing. He never even sat near her at school."

"He go to Bible school with her?"

"No. Ed's Catholic."

"Makes you wonder, huh?"

"What?"

"Well, Ed's the only guy on the team with no motive at all. It's sort of like the guy with the perfect alibi. Makes you suspicious."

"Not me, it doesn't."

He went back to City Hall and I went into the hotel lobby. Hank had turned off the overhead lights and left on the lamp beside the registration counter. It threw a glowing patch across the stippled floor and showed up cigars and boxes on the first shelf under the glass case top.

I went to the foot of the stairs and stood a moment, wondering if Margaret might be awake and decided to make a swing around back to check her light.

The wind was up some, I could hear it overhead, steady and awful enough to make you wonder how come nobody ever worshipped it like they did the sun and rivers. Back when I wrangled beef on the hoof I used to think wind was in charge of it all since it brought the rain and snow, cold and warm, maybe even the dark and light.

I walked around the privy hedge beside the back shed, passed the garage and neared the elms in the L out back. Bertha's light was out but there was a glow from Margaret's window. I wondered if she might be reading or had let her hair down and was brushing it. Then the light went out.

I got the sudden notion that she might come around to the parlor and decided to move, just in case.

My sudden switch from walk to run threw off his blow, which instead of flattening me as planned, only sent me rolling in the gravel. I was still rolling as he jumped, my feet caught his legs, he did a half flip and landed flat on his back. I was up when he tried to rise and laid into him.

Never in my life have I beat a man who wasted so much energy yelling. By the time I had him limp and dragged him around under the light in front, everybody awake within a mile showed up. He was pretty messed up by then but I recognized the voice and the big mouth as Gustafson's. At first the crowd was feeling sorry for him, figuring I'd been overzealous, but when he kept yelling someone suggested I sock him again.

Joey came loping around from City Hall, sent a citizen for Doc and told the rest to go the hell home. Then we hauled Gustafson over to the doc's office. Doc appeared within a few minutes, slightly mussed but complete with tie.

By then Gustafson had stopped yelling and was complaining that there was no damned reason for a man who'd been standing gawking up at the hotel to suddenly take off and run around the garage and then get up when he'd been hit with a roll of dimes which had worked fine when he'd seen a fella pull that stunt in a movie. I told him the dimes would've worked better if he'd used two rolls loose in a sock.

He was thinking about that when Joey asked if I wanted to sign an assault complaint. I said no thanks but maybe we could jail the dumb son of a bitch for gross stupidity. Joey said that was no crime. I thought about that some and decided he was probably right. If it was most of our lawmakers would be in the pokey.

Gustafson headed back for the hotel and I stood on the street corner with Joey, smoking a cigarette and staring at our dead town. The only cars in sight were parked around the hotel and the only action was a couple survivor bugs around the streetlight.

"I guess Otte's sleeping alone," said Joey.

"Far as I know. His partner's gone and he's hardly had time to pick up a floozy."

He sighed and asked would I fix up a cot for him in the hall beside Otte's door.

"We charge three bucks for cots in hunting season," I said.

He gave me a look that made me grin and admit I was willing to make an exception in his case.

All the time he was hoping I'd agree to use the cot but I didn't.

He was getting paid more to protect the citizenry and besides, what could be worse in this world than to set yourself up outside a man's room to protect him and then find him dead in the morning? It was a chance I wasn't about to take.

TWENTY-TWO

Joey told me later he heard Otte use the thundermug twice in the night and pace the floor between times. When he came out in the morning and found Joey sitting up on the cot, he looked more stunned than surprised. Later, in the lobby, he looked like death defrosted.

He was taking the train back home because relatives of Jacobson were driving the car he'd rented to California and said they had no room for him.

Joey and I walked to the depot and we watched guys load Jacobson's coffin on the baggage car before Otte climbed aboard. He stood on the top step, staring gloomily at us.

"I hope you dumb bastards get the guy that killed Phil," he said. "He was okay. My best goddamn friend in the world."

"You still got no ideas?" I asked.

"Only Titus makes any sense, and he's too damned old to take those guys."

"They weren't outmuscled," I said.

He shook his head and leaned out for a last look west toward Main. The train jerked easy, then began to move.

"Well," said Otte, "see you."

We nodded, knowing he wouldn't ever again, and watched him move inside the car and out of sight.

"If the killer did those guys because of what they did to Bunny," said Joey as we headed back west, "why wouldn't he have done Otte first since he was the one supposed to have hurt her that night?"

"Maybe he picked the targets on how easy they were to get at. Or maybe in the order that Bunny liked them."

He liked the second idea best but wasn't sold on either and decided it wasn't worth pushing.

"How you going to work things today?" he asked.

"I'll ride with Parker and stick close. Make sure he's never alone."

"You got a shotgun?"

"I'll carry Elihu's four-ten."

"You'll never get a bird with that. You can't shoot for shit."

"How do you know? I've never tried."

He snorted.

"Anyway," I said, "I'm not going along to get birds and the four-ten'll do fine against a slingshot if it comes to that."

"It comes to that, our killer don't have to stick with any slingshot."

That had occurred to me and it wasn't a lot of comfort.

"All I can do," I said, "is make it tough for him."

The Parkers and Bertrands were in the dining room eating breakfast when we took a table near them. Parker asked if Otte got off okay and we nodded. I could see Florine hadn't slept too well but Pat was fresh and ready. Muggsy looked mostly thoughtful and some down. With a mouth as wide as his that could turn New Year's Eve into a wake.

"I hope Otte makes it to the coast," he said.

"If he doesn't," remarked Pat, "Abe had ought to be safe."

Joey didn't appreciate the lightness of that and said, "We don't know only one killer's involved."

It wasn't a remark made to reassure anybody and if he meant it to scare them it worked fine. Even Pat turned solemn.

"If it's okay with you," I told Parker, "I'd like to ride in your car."

"Fine," he said. "You coming along, Joey?"

"I been up all night, you don't mind, I'll get some sleep."

"This is all crazy," said Florine. Her mouth was tight and her eyes burned. "You keep acting as if nothing had happened and insist on going out to murder birds with two men dead and reason to think you're next. If you had an ounce of sense we'd get in that car and go home.

"I can't turn tail and run," said Abe.

"So I can sit in this miserable dump all day and wait for them to haul your body back, right?"

"You didn't have to come on the trip. It was your own damned idea. Now Turner's gone, the bloom's off, right?"

"Well, since you put it so sweetly, yes, it is. He brought the only excitement this town ever saw—"

"Turner," said Abe, biting off each word, "was a dumb turd that chased every twitchy in sight. You were too damn dumb to figure out you were only one of the million he tried to lay, just another notch in the old gun."

She went white and clinched her fists tight. Her first attempt to speak didn't work, then she swallowed, squinted and leaned forward.

"Maybe," she said cheerfully, "you have good reason not to worry about being the next victim."

Parker's eyes flickered toward Joey, then me and back to his wife as his face reddened. "What the hell're you trying to say?"

She'd shaken him and her fists relaxed as she sat back and smiled. "You know perfectly well."

"Well now," said Joey, "let's not get worked up here—"

"By God," yelled Parker, "by *God!* Next I suppose you'll tell these guys I left the room at five Friday morning, is that next?"

"I wouldn't know if you left the room," she said sweetly. "I sleep heavily in the morning. Who knows what you were doing?"

"How about Jacobson," I asked. "Did he make a pass at you?"

"Everybody makes passes at her," yelled Parker. "She asks for it. I'll bet she even tried you, right?"

She came to her feet so quick her chair fell over backward and slammed to the floor. "I don't have to take this. I've had enough!"

She ran for the stairs and raced up. Pat gave us all a glare and followed. Parker looked as if he was going to follow too but then slumped back and sulked.

"How about it?" I asked. "Did Jacobson make a pass?"

"That was a long time ago," said Muggsy.

"You're a big help, pal," said Parker and when Muggsy looked hurt his friend sat forward and patted his forearm. "It's okay. Might's well have it all out. Yeah, Jacobson and Florrie were cozy once, but like he says, it was a long time ago and I never figured anything really happened. All it did was cause a little fight between me and Florine. I never mixed with Jacobson and we went our ways and that was it. Nothing happened here. Fact is, Florrie's a tease, doesn't mean a thing. Always been the belle and can't help trying to keep it up. I tried to kill every son of a bitch she's flirted with, I'd have knocked off more guys than Samson."

Nobody said anything for a few seconds and then Parker sighed and looked at Joey. "If it's okay with you, I'm going up and talk with her."

Joey nodded and he left. Muggsy went too.

"I don't believe it," said Joey.

"That he killed Turner and Jacobson?"

"That's right."

"Neither do I. If he hasn't killed her, he's never going to kill anybody."

TWENTY-THREE

"How come," said Bertha with her mean-eyed squint, "you were horsing around in the back lot last night?"

I sat down at the table by the windows and said I didn't know what she was talking about.

"Horsefeathers. You know exactly. When you got into that fracas with Gustafson. What were you doing out there to begin with?"

"Having a look around."

"Trying to peek in windows?"

"Sure. Standing on tiptoe I can see right into your second-story window real easy."

"If you were looking at any window, it wasn't mine. Let me tell you, Mr. Alley Cat, you ever come sneaking up our stairs I'll smash you like a bedbug."

"God knows you got the heft, dearie."

"You beat up on that poor man because he was mooning around after Margaret, that's what happened, isn't it?"

"You got it all wrong. He swung on me. He admitted that to Joey, God and everybody. Carried along a roll of dimes to do the job."

"Too bad he didn't have a slingshot."

Margaret laughed and Bertha eased off and grinned.

"You two are awful," said Margaret. "Anybody didn't know you, they'd think you had a feud going."

When Margaret finished her coffee she said she was going over to order groceries and I walked through the dining room and hall with her.

"I was hoping you'd drop around last night," I said.

"Were you out in back, planning to toss pebbles at my window?"

"I wanted to see if you were still up."

"And found Gustafson there."

"He must've tailed me. He was waiting by the garage when I started back. I was thinking maybe you were on your way down so I started off in a hurry."

She stopped in the hallway before we reached the lobby entrance.

"I'm glad you were thinking about me."

"I haven't thought of much else."

"Except Florine and Pat Bertrand."

I shook my head. She glanced back down the hall and suddenly reached up and touched my cheek.

"Maybe, if things are quiet tonight, I'll visit again."

"Allright!"

"But only if I'm sure it's safe."

"How safe you got to be?"

She only smiled.

"You don't come to me," I said, "I'll have to come to you."

"Don't do that. I couldn't stand to see you squashed."

She patted my cheek and went out the side door.

In the lobby Hank gave me a thoughtful look and shook his head. "I don't know how you do it."

"It's all in the eyes," I confessed. "One's a little off and it hypnotizes them."

"There's something off somewhere."

We heard a car out front and both gawked through the window as Bud Kinman drove up and parked just south of Bull Dickey's car. He got out, walked around to the passenger side and opened the door for Mrs. Jasperson, the farmer's wife. She was wearing a gray coat, a black hat with a broad brim and shiny new black shoes. Kinman gently took her elbow and guided her toward the front door while she clutched a small black purse in both hands. She wore no rings.

Kinman gave me a defiant eye and asked was there a room for the lady. I looked at her and met the bright blue eyes. Her plain face glowed, the mouth had softened and she looked ten years younger than I remembered her from the farm kitchen the day before.

"You decided," I said.

"It was easy," she told me. "My husband deserted me."

She couldn't have said that more proudly if she'd announced she was marrying the King of England.

"You mean his mother didn't die?"

"Oh yes, she died all right. But when he got there he decided he didn't want to come back. He sent a wire."

"You got a room?" repeated Kinman.

"You're in luck. The guy in eleven checked out this morning. She can have that."

Kinman suddenly grinned. He had great teeth and I was glad I hadn't had to punch him in the mouth.

"I told you it'd be all right," he said to Mrs. Jasperson and she glowed at him.

"You got any luggage?" I asked.

They both looked rattled and then he hustled out to the car with Hank close behind and opened the trunk.

"I'm glad for you," I told the lady.

"Thank you, you're very kind. I didn't think you would be when you came to the house but by the time you left, I knew you weren't bad."

"Well, don't pass it around, you'll ruin my reputation."

Hank and Kinman returned with three suitcases and hauled them upstairs. The lady trailed them.

I sat down, feeling faintly like Cupid for no good reason I could imagine, and rolled a cigarette. Hank returned, wanting to know what that was all about and I told him what I knew.

"Well," he said, "I don't think he's going to be sleeping in two tonight."

"No, and he probably won't go hunting either. I've got a hunch his buddies'll be busing back home."

TWENTY-FOUR

The football crowd had decided the night before where they were going to hunt but I didn't catch on to the location until we were approaching the white farm house on a hill several miles south and a jog west from Corden. It was the old Grafton place, where I'd lost a friend and killed a man. I'd liked to have suggested another spot but since I was only along as a bodyguard and an uninvited one at that, it didn't seem likely my squeamishness would go over well so I kept still.

It was about as bad as I'd guessed it would be. I got some kick out of their rituals, like when they went through a fence. Two guys would pry the top and second wire strands apart and guys would duck through one at a time after handing their shotguns to a partner who'd hand it back when they were through.

I figured it was a drill worked out by Bull but they said they learned it from their pas, who, for all they knew, got it from their grandfathers. I doubted that, since pheasants hadn't made it over from China to South Dakota that far back.

When we reached the target field Bull and Ed took Phil's car and drove to the opposite end of the field just inside the tree windbreak while the rest of us spread out and hiked through the stubble corn trying to scare up birds. Parker walked the left flank and I stayed on his right. Muggsy took the far right flank, which surprised me some until I learned later they figured flankers got the most good shots and had been working it that way for years.

The ground was frozen but lumpy. That meant we didn't build up layers of mud on our boots but it also made stumbling a regular thing and it's tiring as hell. I never worked much harder trying to have fun and realized the reason Scandinavians thought it was a great sport was because it was such hard work.

I kept Parker in sight all the way: hunting, through lunch and even piss call. He pretended it was annoying but didn't make any effort to cut me loose. Nobody I could notice hung around; even Muggsy kept his distance.

Parker missed two birds he thought he should've had and nailed a third. The rest of the gang got three between them. I never fired a shot and wished I'd left the damned shotgun at the hotel.

Late in the afternoon we covered the longest cornfield in South Dakota without seeing anything but a crow who jeered at us from out of range. Back at the car Waterboy broke out two pints of whiskey and everybody, even Bull, took a swig and unloaded shotguns. It seemed to lift spirits, particularly Parker's. He started kidding Waterboy about his progress from the punk who hauled water to the man with the flask.

"The real reason that dumb team did so fine," said Waterboy, "was that I spiked the pail before every game."

"Go on, we'd have tasted it."

"Like hell. I filtered it. What I did was, I got tanked each night before a game, pissed in the pail in the morning and you dumb jocks never noticed a thing. You were so scared before every game I could've crapped in the pail and you wouldn't notice. The guys not scared were too busy looking at girls on the sideline to catch on."

Only Titus didn't laugh. He took just one swig from Waterboy's flask and looked tired from the hunt. I suppose we all looked tired, but he was much older. He rode with Parker, Muggsy, Swede and me back to town. Muggsy and Parker talked quietly in the front seat. We in the back stared out across the prairie.

Finally I turned to Titus.

"I hear Swede missed a lot of practice because his old man made him work."

Titus nodded. "Swede was the only guy on the team thought my training schedule was easy. Football was a breeze compared to working for old man Eckerson."

Swede nodded without a smile. I asked him how young he was when he started to work. He said he couldn't remember that far back.

"But you went to Bible school."

"That was before he was fully grown," said Titus. "His ma got her way on that one. Probably the only time in her life when she did."

"You like Bible school?" I asked.

"Yah, it was fine."

"Bull was in that class too, right?"

He nodded. "And Jacobson and Otte."

"And Marlis Nelson and Bunny," I said.

He nodded again.

"How'd Bull and Bunny get along?"

"Fine."

"Was Bull watching out for her then too?"

He frowned and said he didn't know what I meant. I told him I'd heard he seemed to feel responsible for her, tried to keep her from getting into trouble.

"I don't know about any of that. If that's what he tried, he wasn't much good at it."

"You think he made a play for her?"

He shrugged and said he'd certainly been around a lot.

Back at the hotel Joey met us in front and looked relieved at the sight of a healthy Parker. Parker grinned at him and swaggered a little.

"You didn't think I'd make it," he said.

"I worried some," admitted Joey.

"Your old buddy stayed so close I thought he was gonna shake it for me when I took a leak."

"Well," said Joey, looking my way, "he did his job."

"Ah, he just figures on getting in good with Florine," said Parker. "I'm gonna get out of these damn boots and go get me a drink. You think Hank'd take our birds over to the butcher for dressing?" he asked me.

"He's in the lobby," I said. "Ask him."

The locals went their way and the rest trooped into the lobby while I stayed with Joey on the sidewalk.

"Anything interesting happen?" he asked.

"No."

"How'd you like hunting?"

"It's horseshit."

"You'd like it better if you did some shooting."

"Yeah, like traveling'd be better if you didn't have to go anywhere. I guess you got your beauty sleep."

"I'll be able to keep an eye on Parker's room tonight."

I was happy to hear that, figuring it might make it possible for me to enjoy Margaret.

He wanted to know if I'd noticed anybody trying to get close to Parker during the hunt.

"It was more like they were afraid he'd draw lightning. I had him to myself all day."

Joey shook his head. "I just can't believe any of those guys'd kill."

"None of 'em were shy about killing birds."

He didn't find that worth comment.

TWENTY-FIVE

Hank ate dinner with Bertha and I had mine with Margaret. I marveled more than ever that Bertha still liked Margaret even though the woman encouraged me. We sat in the booth alcove just off the kitchen and were left alone.

I asked Margaret if Gustafson had bothered her any and she told me he spent the day resting and getting a chipped tooth repaired and finding out if he was going to lose one I'd loosened during our debate.

"How well'd you know him in Iowa?" I asked.

"I saw him at dances a few times, and in cafés."

"Dance with him?"

"A couple times."

"Is that all?"

"I never took him to bed, if that's what you're after."

"I'm not after anything except some idea of why he tried to come on so strong. He know about what happened to Bunny?"

"There were times I thought everybody in South Dakota knew, but actually I'm not sure. Word got around that she was pregnant without a husband. About a year after she died, I became sort of a target for a lot of men around town. A reasonably young widow with no man brings out something in certain types."

I knew just what it was and tried to think how I could ask if she put out a lot even while I figured what the hell was it to me. I'd never cared before how busy a woman was before I showed up.

"I can't figure this Gustafson guy," I admitted to her. "He just doesn't seem a guy you'd go for but he acts like he had a claim. You know what I'm trying to say?"

"He had no kind of claim on me," she said firmly. "He's just one of those men who think they've a right to women from their territory wherever they may be. I also suspect he felt I had come down rather far in the world if I accepted a job as a scullion in a hotel like this and would be vulnerable. And a man like you makes him all the worse. He simply had to beat you and then you humiliated him and it makes him crazy."

"He come around to see you when he got back from the dentist?"

"I saw him in the lobby. He sat down across from me there and talked a little. He said he hadn't meant anything that first evening, just wanted to be friendly and thought I was shy."

"That was it?"

"Just about. He offered to help me if I needed anything and when I assured him I needed nothing he could offer he wished me well and said he'd be leaving in the morning if his friend Downer agreed."

"Can you come down to the parlor tonight?" I asked.

She glanced toward the kitchen and frowned.

"I think it'd be foolish. Joey will be here again, won't he?"

"Just upstairs."

"I don't care to depend on that. Anyway, Parker will only be here another couple days. When he's gone, it might all be different."

I've always been long on eager and short on patience so the stalling off didn't appeal but when I tried to push she got up, cleared the table and moved back to the kitchen with Bertha.

After dinner I kept close to Parker at the beer parlor and later watched him playing poker in the dining room with Bull, Ed Folsum, Muggsy and Waterboy. Swede didn't show up and Waterboy told us his wife was fed up with his partying. She tolerated the hunting because she liked pheasant but couldn't hold still for him having fun with beer and cronies.

Bull shook his head. "If she realized how little fun he has I suspect she'd not object."

"Come on," said Waterboy, "he has fun, it's just not allowed to show."

Parker told Waterboy it was his goddamned turn to bet and everybody tried to concentrate on the game for a while. It went badly for Parker. He kept getting second-best hands and trying to push them. Waterboy won noisily, Bull was close but quiet.

"Be happy," Waterboy told Parker while raking in another pot, "you been lucky in love."

Parker's face turned red but he kept quiet with obvious effort and Bull scowled at Waterboy.

They folded up the game a little after eleven. Florine and Pat were in the lobby, talking about a movie they'd gone to earlier. Hank had been listening to Florine's account of it and she was aglow from his rapt attention. I saw Parker scowl and guessed she'd be catching it for trying to rob the cradle. Hank's disappointment at the interruption was a little too obvious and Waterboy didn't help when he grinned and said Florine had made another conquest.

"Yeah," said Parker, "she's great with the junior league."

Florine went up the stairs ahead of him and from the look she handed over before turning away, I guessed he'd be lucky if she didn't have a slingshot hidden in her undies.

I went over to the register to check on people and found that Kinman's gang had checked out.

When I looked at Hank he grinned.

"What happened?" I asked.

"The guys went. Kinman's still here with his lady. He's still got room two but I don't think he's been anywhere but in eleven. It's lucky Grandma's not dead."

That went by me and I said so.

"Well, if she were, she'd be spinning in her grave like a drill head."

Joey showed up, saving me from the problem of following that remark and wanting to know if everyone was tucked away. I said they were that or close. He went upstairs, prowled the halls and came back. Hank wished us both good night and left.

"You want the cot up there again?" I asked Joey.

He nodded and sat in the rocker beside the register alcove.

"You know any way we could check to see if Otte stayed on the train to California?" I asked.

His eyes opened wide. "You got a notion?"

"I just wonder. He was the guy that spoiled the party. It just seems like the other guys might've been kind of sore about that."

He got up and headed for the stairs. A few minutes later he came back with Parker behind him. When they were seated Joey leaned toward him.

"What'd you, Jacobson and Turner do when Otte hurt Bunny?"

"What'd you think? We hauled him off."

"I want to know just exactly what the hell happened. Now you tell me and don't be cute."

It took a while but gradually it all came out. Otte had wanted to do her different because all the others had been in first and so he lifted and turned her and she didn't like that and wanted to know what he was doing and he tried to tell her she'd like it but she fought and finally Otte tried to go in the back door and she screamed. Turner had grabbed Otte by the hair and hauled him out of the car and when Otte tore loose and elbowed him in the gut, Parker and Jacobson had jumped in. They worked him over pretty good and let him know they thought he was eight kinds of an asshole.

Parker finished that story hunched over, holding his hands clinched together and his head down.

"He bawled. Not because he was hurt, but because we ganged up on him. It was a hell of a night, I'll tell you."

"So how'd it end?" asked Joey.

"We three guys and Bunny drove back to town and left Otte to hike it. Bunny wouldn't stay in the car if he was in it and Turner backed her up. I wasn't too happy about that but went along."

We were all silent for a few seconds before I finally asked how come if it was that bitter, Jacobson and Otte wound up in California together.

"Otte had an uncle running a business out there and he knew the two guys had been pals and offered jobs to both of them. The money was good and they just naturally forgot the trouble after a while and acted like nothing bad ever happened."

"There was no talk about it at the reunion?"

"Hell no." He straightened up wearily. "Shit, it was ten years ago, Bunny was gone. You don't hang on to bad times, you talk about the good ones."

"And you don't think Otte held a grudge?"

"I don't think he ever forgave Turner, but he never liked him much to start. He never acted standoffish with me and he was really pals with Jacobson. If Turner was the only one killed, I might wonder, but I'm damned sure Otte never would've killed Jacobson. Never."

I remembered how Otte seemed to forget about my busting his tail and felt inclined to agree it didn't seem likely he was the kind to hold a ten-year grudge. On the other hand, I'd never been his great old buddy like the others had and that could put a different slant on the whole business.

Parker went back to his loving wife and Joey asked me to keep an eye on his door while he went over to City Hall and made some telephone calls. I knew it would pain him to spend town money for long distance but he was desperate enough to overrule his natural stingy streak.

He came back half an hour later saying he hadn't been able to get any satisfaction but he'd follow up in the morning. Meanwhile he'd watch Parker.

By then the guests were silent and the prairie wind moaned over us and made the hotel creak and mutter. I went out into it, felt the cold against my face and walked the streets near the hotel, looking for strange cars or meandering citizens.

There was nothing doing.

I returned to the parlor, slipped off my shoes and stretched out on the couch, wondering about Kinman and his lady, how come they stayed on. Probably he was leery about bringing his love back to the hometown. He would no doubt have to set her up in an apartment until they could get properly married since he ran a store and depended on folks who had firm ideas about the proprieties. I thought too of trying to persuade him in the morning that he should quit pretending he still slept in two so I could rent it out to other hunters.

The first sound outside the parlor lifted my hopes; I guessed it was Margaret slipping down the hall. Then I realized the sound didn't come from the hall. I lifted my head, heard only the wind and sat up. There it was again. A scraping sound. I rose, sneaked to the front window and saw a foot disappear over the balcony edge to my left.

I was out the door and up the stairs faster than a cat with a kerosened ass. Joey jerked erect as I grabbed his shoulder, then his head and whispered in his ear: "Somebody's on the balcony. We go in, catch him coming through the window—okay?"

He nodded. I knew the door wouldn't be locked because there was no key for it and Parker'd been too proud to object. All I feared was Parker or Florine'd wake and scream but they both slept, snoring softly as I moved to the window on stocking feet and put my back against the wall on the right. Joey took the left.

For several seconds we heard nothing and I wondered if I'd been dreaming. Then the window squeaked faintly and began to lift. When it was well up, there was a long moment of waiting.

Then a head appeared, facing the bed. After a second, it withdrew. I thought we'd lost him and was about to move in pursuit when a leg came through, followed by its owner, all bent low to scrape under the sill.

I said, "Okay," and we grabbed for him.

Joey missed his right arm, took an elbow to the gut and went to his knees. I tried to twist the arm I grabbed but he butted me between the eyes with his forehead and I saw lights and lost my grip. The next second he was at the door, jerked it open and charged into the hall. I stumbled on my first step, got momentum and went after him.

He took the steps two at a jump, I did three and landed on his back when he hit bottom. He rolled, I hung on to his wrist and went along till we hit the wall, then let go quick and scrambled to my feet. He came in a bull rush, I skipped aside, kicked his shin, clipped his head with my fist and watched him hit the door with his head. He landed in a heap and before he could pull together I spun him over, got his arms in a double lock and had him looking like a turkey ready for the oven.

Joey came down and cuffed the prisoner's wrists.

"Well," he said, "I wasted money on the long-distance calls."

Swede lifted his glazed eyes to stare at me as we lifted him erect and I patted his pockets.

"I don't find a slingshot," I said.

"Don't worry. He dropped it on the bedroom floor when we grabbed him," said Joey.

TWENTY-SIX

We took Swede over to City Hall, parked him in the little cell and tried to question him. He sat on the iron cot with his big farmer hands dangling between his knees and his elbows resting on his thighs, looking dazed. I could see a red lump on the top of his head where the hair was thin, but there was no blood.

"I'm gonna call Doc," Joey said. "You be all right?"

I nodded.

He closed the door behind him but didn't lock it. I didn't think Swede noticed.

"You never got over her, did you?" I said.

He stared at the floor.

"When'd it start? While you two were in Bible school together?"

He looked toward the cell door and I wondered if he had paid attention when Joey left.

"Was it your wife's idea?" I asked. "Was she the one figured those guys had to be punished?"

He looked at me.

"A friend of Bunny's told me you fell in love with Bunny when you were just kids and that she loved back."

"Her name was Bonita," he said.

"I forgot."

He nodded. "Bonita Angela. She never told anybody else that."

I let him remember for a while as he stared into space. Then he looked at me again. "Now what?" he asked.

"It depends. Why'd you kill Turner first?"

His eyes closed, he swallowed and stared at his hands.

"He took her away."

"And Jacobson?"

"He did it to her with the others and I had an easy chance at him."

"How about if you'd killed Parker tonight. Would you have gone after Otte in California?"

He shrugged.

"How'd you know Turner'd be taking a shower Saturday morning?"

"He told Waterboy he always took a cold shower after he'd laid with a woman."

"How'd you know he'd been laid that morning?"

He leaned back against the cell wall and braced his hands on the cot.

"I watched Rose's place. Figured he'd go there. He did. Waited till he came out and let him get back to the hotel. Went in the side door there, heard the shower. It was easy."

"You climbed on top the bureau, got your elbows over the partition and shot him with your slingshot while he was soaping up, huh?"

"He was rinsing off."

"Pretty easy shot?"

"Oh yah. When I stretched out my arm he wasn't four feet away. Never opened his eyes. Real easy. I can hit a gopher's head ten feet off. They're lots harder."

"You feel good when he went down?"

"It scared me, he made so much noise falling there. I couldn't stay and watch but he was a goner. Blood shot out—"

"You didn't come down the front stairs?"

"No. I figured you'd wake up. I snuck down the servants' way and then out the east door and went home."

"Where'd you leave your car?"

"Home."

"You walked in and back?"

"Couldn't leave it in town. Somebody'd notice. Joey, more'n likely."

"So your wife knew what you were doing."

"She didn't have nothing to do with any of it. She knew what I had to do, but didn't take any hand."

I wondered at the thought of a woman who'd stand by while her husband avenged the death of a woman he was in love with beyond life.

When Joey came back Doc was with him.

I stood out by the town fire truck watching the cell with Joey while Doc examined our prisoner, and reported what Swede had told me.

"I kind of figured he might unload on you if I stayed away," said Joey. He shook his head. "This is a sorry mess. What's his wife gonna do all alone on that farm with her man in prison?"

"I don't think she'd want me to fill in."

He leaned against the fire truck and frowned at me.

"When'd you decide it was Swede?"

"When I heard Bunny'd had a fella before Turner."

"You seemed to think it was Otte for a while."

"I guess it was more I hoped it wasn't Swede. Otte never really fit. He's not smart enough to be an actor and while he's got a hell of a temper, his memory's short. He couldn't stay mad at me for a half day when I broke his tail, I didn't figure he could carry a grudge ten years just because his buddies slapped him around and left him to walk three miles."

"There was a difference," said Joey. "They were his old

buddies and they turned on him. You were just a guy he had a brawl with."

Doc came out of the cell and Joey went to lock it, then we all went into Joey's office.

"I gave him a sedative," said Doc. "He needs sleep but he's not in too bad shape. Gonna have a stiff neck. What'd you hit him on the head with?" he asked me.

"The door."

He thought that over, decided not to pursue it and left.

"Somebody's gotta go tell Mrs. Eckerson what's happened," said Joey.

"Don't look at me," I said. "If I went and told her, she'd drill me sure."

He sighed, put his hat on, squared it off and tramped out to his car. I put my deputy's badge on his desk and went back to the hotel.